The Virgin and The Veteran

By: Cathy Henn

The Virgin and The Veteran

Available for purchase at:
www.createspace.com/3512624

ISBN-13: 978-1456405342

The cover illustration was created by my son,
Kyle Henn, www.henndesign.net

Many thanks to Frozen Ed, Danger, Winter, and
RawDog for navigational advice, and to Margaret
Cole for her proof-reading skills.

How to contact the author:
Cathy Henn
easternphoebe@gmail.com

Dedicated to *lazarus* and ***RawDog***, veterans of the
Barkley Marathons.
Their lifelong friendship is the inspiration for this
story.

Chapter 1: The Virgin

Early Saturday morning

He and Emmitt lay there in the dry leaves panting. They looked like two tired hound dogs after a long run—tongues out, chests heaving, eyes rolled back in their heads. They were spent and needed a good long rest. But that wasn't going to happen any time soon, not if they wanted their freedom.

"Come on, Emmitt, get up, we've got to get going," he choked out while rolling himself over onto his hands and knees, head still down, long brown hair hanging over his eyes. "They're coming, we've got to go." He grabbed Emmitt's arm where it was thrown out to the side of his spread-eagled, prone body.

Emmitt moaned. "Nooooooo, I can't. You go on without me."

"No, come on, you've got to get up. I ain't leaving you here. The dogs are coming, and they might eat you." Emmitt was deathly afraid of dogs, so he thought this would persuade him. He poked Emmitt in the side and tried to roll him over. Emmitt had hurt his leg in the drop from the wall, and had been hard-pressed to keep up with Clyde in the flight through the forest.

Emmitt just huddled up into a little ball and covered his head with his hands and moaned louder.

"Noooooo, I'm not going any farther. I'd rather die."

But a moment later he uncovered his eyes and peered out at Clyde. "You go on, Clyde. Just leave me here. I'll tell the rest of 'em back in the yard that you didn't give up. We'll all be rooting for you."

He said it with such force, in between gasps of breath, that Clyde was caught up with the push in his words. It was what he needed most to make up his mind. "Okay," he said pensively, squatting on his heels in front of Emmitt. "Are you sure?"

"YES! Go on, get!" Emmitt pushed his shin hard and Clyde plopped awkwardly backwards into the dirt and leaves. He reassembled his body and stood up, snorting in surprise.

"Okay, then," he said in a low voice. *Go on alone*, he thought with apprehension, *out there in the unknown wilderness?* First-time escaped cons like him were called "Virgins" by the more experienced prisoners, and known to get horribly lost or injured before they were recaptured. No one had ever successfully escaped from the prison and made their way through the backwoods on their first try, and only a paltry handful had ever succeeded on successive attempts.

Clyde didn't want to travel alone, but what choice did he have? If he gave up, he'd be back in his cot tonight, or more likely down in the concrete Hole.

2

Chapter 1: The Virgin

No victory in that! Just more pain and misery and yearning. Today was his big chance and there might not be another. He had almost made the decision to go, but he hesitated because he had a foreboding that it was going to be the most frightening adventure of his life. The mountains were treacherous despite their beauty. To take his mind off his fears, he broke off a blade of long grass and chewed on it, then spit it out in a wet wad on the ground.

Clyde turned hesitantly and looked out at the vast green terrain and the blue bowl of a sky. He closed his eyes and breathed it all in for a moment. He took stock of himself mentally. His breathing had slowed and was almost normal. His blue chambray shirt was ripped open in the front and wet and ragged from dragging his body through the briers, and his arms and chest were lacerated and oozing blood from the sharp points in the thorny tunnels he had pushed and pulled himself through. His legs were weary because he had been running all night, and his jeans were ripped and filthy. His stomach was rumbling with hunger, and he rubbed it quiet with his hands. His aching feet, encased in old leather work boots, seemed to argue with him about the wisdom of making them climb more hills. He tried to shut all the complaints off.

It was one of those glorious June mornings when the world just seemed right, and he felt it. He felt the heat of the sun beating upon his arms. The cool touch of the air enveloping him as he began moving through it was intoxicating. He slowly walked up the hill leaving Emmitt lying by the old guard shack, then he looked back, and said one more time, loudly, "Are you sure?!"

Emmitt yelled with conviction, "Get on out of here!"

"Well, then…what the hell…" Clyde said. He shrugged, and acquiesced. It was time to go on alone, to make the mountains before him move out of his way—to find freedom beyond the constraints that held him there.

He started hiking up the hill slowly on the old coal hauling road. He had a hazy plan to keep following the road until it went somewhere, but he wasn't sure where that might be. He hoped it went to the river, because then he thought he could follow the river downstream and maybe lose the dogs that were bound to be hunting him.

He was only about 100 feet away from Emmitt when he heard voices coming up the road towards him. He darted up the hill to the left of the road behind a rocky outcropping, and huddled behind it, listening.

"You always think you're smarter than me, don't you?!" he heard.

Chapter 1: The Virgin

"That's because I am, you dumbass!" Two voices arguing came floating up out of the hollow to where Clyde crouched trembling.

He slowly peeked around the edge of the rocks. Sure enough, it was the Hicks' brothers, two guards at the prison. The manning of the prison was a local affair. Sometimes there would be three generations of men working there. The young men came into the place and were indoctrinated into prison guard life by their elders. The two men heading towards Emmitt were big, burley fellows. They loved their beer, loved their chaw, fought with each other all the time, and were known for their roughness and cruelty to the prisoners.

"Oh no, the Hicks' boys," thought Clyde. "Emmitt is in for it now." He tried to think of how he could rescue Emmitt, but it was too late. The Hicks' brothers walked past him and approached the spot where Emmitt still lay in the dirt. Clyde watched the scene unfold, knowing exactly what was going to go down.

"Lookie there, it's one of them es-kay-pees!" said Hicks brother #1 gleefully. (Clyde never could keep Bubba and Bud straight).

"Yeah!" said Hicks brother #2, excited.

They ran straight to Emmitt, and towered over him menacingly. Emmitt just cowered in the dirt, legs drawn up to his chest, protecting his vitals.

Then the kicking began. It was always the same. They invariably went for the kidneys. A man needed his kidneys to urinate right. When they beat up the kidneys, a body couldn't pee for weeks after without excruciating pain.

"This will teach you, you lousy little creep!" Brother #1 commenced kicking Emmitt's lower back where the kidneys lay quietly beneath, pumping out bloody urine to the bladder with every kick, as the kidney tissue became bruised and bleeding. Brother #1 was 6'4" and 300 pounds, and he was kicking with his big, lug-soled, heavy boots.

Brother #2 started in on the other side, going for Emmitt's knees, arms, and head, and dancing about in an agitated manner between kicks while shouting, "Yee haw!"

The blows crashed into Emmitt, and he was screaming in agony, "Stop! Please! No more, no more!"

Suddenly Brother #1 yanked Emmitt upright like he was throwing a bale of hay onto a wagon, and slammed his back against a tree. Emmitt would have washed down the tree like water into a puddle at the bottom, but Brother #1 held him there by his grip on the front of his shirt, with Emmitt's bruised back pressed into the unyielding oak.

Chapter 1: The Virgin

"Where is he? Where's Clyde? We know he was with you! Where'd he go?" he demanded angrily.

"I dunno," moaned Emmitt.

Brother #2 punched Emmitt in the gut, hard.

Emmitt couldn't double over because Brother #1 kept him upright by his white-knuckled grip on his shirt.

"Which way did he go? Tell us or you'll be hamburger by the time we get you back to the Hole."

Emmitt had been Clyde's cell-mate for a few years. They had bonded when they found out they were both from the same great State of Missouri. There was also a camaraderie between them born of shared extreme hardships. But things were getting out of hand, and Clyde knew Emmitt was not a strong-minded person.

Clyde feared that Emmitt might spew out his direction of travel any moment, so he began to back away from the rocks, crouching close to the ground. When he thought he was out of sound range, he turned and crept away up the wooded hill, tucking in behind every big tree and rock like a soldier in battle mode. After long, fearful moments, he was far enough away to run back down close to the road.

Clyde felt badly about poor Emmitt. He would be in pain for a long time, or dead if the Hicks' brothers didn't let up.

Chapter 2: The Veteran

Friday night

Six. There had been six blasts of the steam whistle, meaning there were six escaped convicts on the loose. Six! He shook his head. Unbelievable. How could the guard in the closest tower have not seen them all going over? And apparently he had only shot the last man, whom they had already recaptured, just moments after he hit the ground. That was one guard who was going to get his ass fired before this was over with, John thought grimly.

It was dusk, and the prison lay deep in a hollow surrounded by heavily forested, inhospitable mountains. Finding their trail was going to be a job and a half, especially if they had all split up.

At the sound of the steam whistle blowing, he had rushed out of the dog kennels and hurried to the front gate. Many of the other guards were already there when he arrived.

"Can't go yet," said Connelly, the guard on duty at the gate. "Got to get orders from the State capital. This is gonna be a big one," he said ominously. "Clyde got out."

John sighed and said, "Well, shit," to no one in particular. The other guards were all shaking their heads and cussing too.

Connelly told them the news about which other prisoners had escaped and how they had made a pipe-ladder to go over the wall. Then they all stood around impatiently waiting for their orders. Evidently the State didn't think the guards could handle the job by themselves, and they were gathering up their resources to send to the backwoods prison. The guards were pissed off and everyone was anxious to get going.

Finally, the orders came through by telephone, and the gate opened to let them out. They rushed to the scene of the escape at the back of the prison. The place was a pool of frustrated inactivity, with off-duty guards and locals milling about, talking back and forth with the guards on the wall. Bright beacons of light were shining down from the walls, illuminating the area around the prison. No one had left the vicinity to look for the cons' trail yet. They were waiting for someone to give them orders.

John, as the Director of Security, was the one in charge. He strode up to the group and said, "Let's go, men." They immediately split up into twos and began combing the area behind the northeast corner of the yard wall in the area where the cons had dropped. They circled anxiously like dogs who had lost the trail.

"Here!" yelled out Hammond. Hammond had been a guard at the prison for over forty years, and hadn't lost his acumen yet. John ran to his side. Hammond was pointing to something in the weeds. It was spatters of blood. John reached down and touched one spot, and it was still wet. He wiped his fingers off on his tough work jeans.

"Looks like we've got another wounded con. He won't get far." he said to Hammond and his partner McPeters.

"Ought to be easy to track," the young McPeters piped up.

"He's a goner," declared Hammond.

"Yep," agreed John. "Good job. Keep looking," he said.

There was another call from farther down the wall. It was Wilson this time. Wilson was a local fellow who they sometimes allowed to help with man-hunts because he was good in the woods and energetic. John tried to ignore his unkempt appearance. It looked like he never cut his hair or shaved, and he wore cut-off blue jeans and an old t-shirt with one of those hippie peace symbols on it.

"What'd ya find, Steve?" he asked.

"See this here branch? It's bent and broken like somebody was holding it back for somebody else, nice-like."

"Hmmm. Who'd be nice enough to do that?" John asked.

"Clyde," said Wilson emphatically.

"Probably holding it back for Emmitt," John said, thinking about Clyde's sickly cellmate, Emmitt. "He's always taking care of him like he was his mother."

John found some more blood splatters nearby. "So, I think we know that Clyde and Emmitt went up this creek bed. Maybe the other three did, too. Why don't you two hike up there about 100 yards and watch for a spell?" He motioned for two guards to come closer and pointed to a dark area up the hill. The two guards knew to go there and lay quietly like deer hunters waiting for deer to come by. They would hardly move a muscle, laying in the dark waiting for a noise.

John thought that possibly Clyde and Emmitt were sitting a ways up the creek bed, in the darkness, listening and waiting to see what would happen. They might come back down in a little while and seek an easier route.

But they might be easy prey right where they were. He'd better get on up there and look. He moved quietly over to Stockstill, his buddy and second in command, who appeared to be deep in concentration as he paced his area, twirling one side

12

of his long mustache around his index finger over and over.

"Got to go check out this creek gully," John said quietly. "You take over down here 'til I get back. You know the routine."

"No prob," said Harry Stockstill, not even looking up. "Good luck," he said after a second or two.

Harry rarely had a lot to say, and when he did converse, he usually measured his words out like precious gold dust. John liked that reserve about him, considering him to be a smart and resourceful kind of guy.

"If I'm not back in 30 minutes, send Wilson and Whitey up after me with Blue and Punkin," John said in a low voice, referring to two of his best dogs. Blue and Punkin were his most experienced bloodhounds.

"Sure," said Harry.

"Don't let anybody take Sassy or Elvis out. We'll save them for the final chase," he said, referring to his two newly trained young bloodhounds.

"Yep," said Harry knowingly.

John went back to the creek bed and started up it, solo. There was a rushing rivulet of water coming down it. He could walk as quietly as a barefoot

Indian, and see as well as a barred owl zoning in on its prey. He almost never needed his headlamp, even though he always carried it in his backpack. He hoped to sneak up on the two fugitives.

After thirty minutes of rock hopping through the creek, he realized they were not waiting in hiding after all, but were set upon reaching the mountaintop. He thought about going back to get his dogs, but then he would lose an hour, and the escaped cons might be too far ahead. So he kept climbing.

John was a veteran of many manhunts for escaped convicts. He had a reputation for always bringing back his man. He had great confidence in his abilities, and he knew he would not fail. The search for these cons was going to be different, though. The whole country was going to be in an uproar, because Clyde had killed someone important. That meant the FBI would be coming, the State Troopers, the SWAT teams, the helicopters, and the reporters. John knew the drill. They would come into his territory and try to take over the search. He had to hurry and find his man before the outsiders messed everything up with their lack of experience and sloppy techniques.

He knew where this creek went from hundreds of coon hunting trips at night. The head of it was a steep 700 feet up near an old abandoned coal mine and prisoner camp, with a coal hauling road leading out. If he continued up from there, he would reach a second old coal hauling road, and then veering to the northwest 400 more feet he would be at another abandoned prisoner-worked coal mine. 500 feet more and he would be on the top of the mountain, with access to the road going down the other side through the State's natural area into civilization. Of course, there were many other options along the way. The cons might find a hiding spot somewhere and hole up for the rest of the night, or if they had any brains at all, they might decide to give up when the terrain got too tough. The wounded man would be a sorry liability for the rest of the group, and probably be left behind in their panic to escape recapture.

He wondered how far they would make it before they gave up.

Chapter 3: The Virgin's Travels

Friday evening, night, and Sat. morning

"Come on Clyde, leave him," said Lester. "Come with us. We're going to head for the highway and steal a car from some dang local. We'll be drinking beer tonight!"

Clyde was well-liked by the other prisoners, and not just because of the crime that had put him behind the wall. He was naturally easy-going and friendly.

"Yeah! We'll find us some pretty women!" hissed Fred.

The five anxious men were huddled up in the thick woods just beyond the prison wall. The evening light was waning, and tree shadows were pooling about them, making the forest seem dark and foreboding. The fear of the unknown crept into their brains, and they felt an urgent need to be running. They had to get on their way quickly, but the decision had not been made beforehand about their direction of travel if they actually succeeded in escaping.

Clyde was longing for some fun, and the thought of ice-cold beer was enticing. He imagined golden beer foaming in a tall frosted glass as it was poured, and then lifting it up and letting it wash down his eager throat. Swallowing, burping. He liked just about any kind of beer, but the dark, amber kinds were his favorites if he had any money. When he didn't, he settled for just about anything.

But he had already decided where to go, long ago when he was pacing in the prison yard, searching the landscape beyond the prison for a route of escape. He was determined to climb the tall mountain that stood behind the north prison wall, even if he had to do it all alone. Hoary Head was what the guards called it, because of the perpetual hoar frost that covered the peak in the winter.

"You know the highway's going to be loaded with guards. We're going over the mountain. They'll never guess anyone tried that way," Clyde said.

"Over the mountain? You'll never make it!" Lester said in surprise.

Clyde shrugged his shoulders and grinned. "You never know."

"Okay, dumbass. See ya on the other side," snickered Lester. He and the other two cons scurried off together through the twilight shadows, keeping hidden in the woods. They would try their luck with the highway, if they could find it.

"Emmitt, let's go," Clyde said.

"I can't," Emmitt whined from his fetal position on the ground.

"Yes, you can. Now get your skinny ass up and let's go," directed Clyde.

Clyde was anxious to climb the looming mountain. It had dominated his vision every day when he went out into the prison yard. Even when he was playing basketball, he was aware of its massive presence in his peripheral view. He imagined himself climbing to the top and proclaiming his innocence to the world from its lofty heights. The mountain stared back at him, challenging him to come on and do his best.

He began a daily conversation with it. "I'm gonna climb you one day," he told it.

"Nooooooo," came back in the wind.

"Yes, I am!" he reiterated.

"You'll die, die, die," screamed the crows flying down into the prison yard from a night on the mountain.

Now here was his chance. He had finally made it over the wall and was at the base of the mountain, free at last to climb it. Except for his wounded companion Emmitt, he would be racing up its side.

Emmitt tried to keep up as they maneuvered their way through the darkness up the rocky creek bed, but his leg hurt where he had been shot when he jumped off the twelve foot tall prison wall.

Chapter 3: The Virgin's Travels

"Hurts bad! I can't hardly make it. It's broke, ain't it?" he beleaguered Clyde. Then his foot slipped off a large moss-covered rock into the icy cold waters of the creek. He had been trying to jump from one rock to another, but miscalculated. He fell backwards onto his butt in the rushing water, and was immediately soaked to his waist. Clyde had to give him a hand to help him get back up.

"Watch your step. Your leg ain't broke. If it was, you wouldn't be walkin' at all. Come on, hurry up," said Clyde impatiently.

Emmitt tried to hurry, but he was so weary. Clyde wheedled and threatened to no avail. Emmitt was not in as good a shape as he was. Their daily activities differed considerably. Clyde played a lot of basketball in the prison yard while Emmitt preferred playing a guitar with the prison band.

"I can't see. It's too dark! I want to go back," wailed Emmitt.

"What? We just got out! Now you want to go back?" said an increasingly irritated Clyde.

Clyde kept trying to verbally goad him into continuing onward up the tortuous path of the creek bed. Emmitt kept slipping and sliding off the rocks into the water and moaning about his leg hurting. At least the frequent dunks in the icy water washed away his blood trail.

After a while, they ran out of creek bed. They had reached the headwaters of the creek, where the cold water bubbled out of a spring in the ground into a small pool. The moon had risen in full force and shone like a sentinel above them. Clyde and Emmitt bent down and scooped up a few welcome swallows of the refreshing water in their palms.

They continued trekking up the mountainside, but it was so steep that they had to stop and rest every thirty minutes or so. It was slow going with Emmitt perpetually lagging behind. It became totally dark in the thick layers of understory, and they lost their bearings entirely. They wandered slowly on for hours, slogging upwards through bushy undergrowth, but sometimes retreating downhill when the way became impassable. They finally came upon an abandoned underground coal mine like a black cave in the hillside, with a locked rusty gate across the opening. They rested in the leaves in front of the gate for a while, then they continued upward.

The mountain was unyielding in its steepness, and Emmitt finally could not handle it another minute. He stopped and sat down on a rock and would not budge. Clyde scouted to the left and right of where he sat, and suggested they cut to the left, where the going looked a little bit easier. They meandered this way and that in the woods, drifting from tree to tree, not sure which way to go.

Chapter 3: The Virgin's Travels

When Emmitt started complaining again, and threatened to give up, they attempted to backtrack over to their resting place at the old coal mine, and eventually found it. Again, they rested in the drift of dead leaves. This time, Clyde discovered an old roadbed hidden in the overgrown vegetation that led away from the mine, and they set out down it, but Clyde did not like being out on a road of any kind. They saw an opening above the road where the moonlight was shining down, and made their way over a pile of rocks to it, curious. The opening in the forest was created by a power-line right-of-way that went straight up the mountain. They looked up it, and Emmitt balked like a tired mule being ordered to pull a heavy load.

"No, please, not that way," he moaned, staring at the face of the nearly perpendicular mountainside. There were high bluffs of rock outlined in the moonlight, with dark, jagged fractures waiting to be climbed.

Clyde was tired of trying to push Emmitt up the mountain. He reluctantly but temporarily gave up his quest to climb Hoary Head. "Okay, we'll go down for now," he sighed. "Maybe there'll be another way up later on."

The way down turned out to be worse than going up. The path was choked with eight foot tall thorny blackberry thickets and tangled viny plants that had half-inch long protruding briers. They could have descended through the forest, but Clyde decided to wade directly into the thicket of briers, thinking to throw off any man-hunters with bloodhounds. Who would take a dog through that? It would be insanely stupid.

They slowly and agonizingly crawled through the thorny tunnels of briers, ripping their shirts and bare skin to shreds. The claw-like thorns dug into the muscles of their shoulders as if the mountain itself was trying to hold them back. There was no way to hurry. Emmitt began crying and whimpering in abject misery. Clyde was sick of his belly-aching, and tried to ignore him, but his persistent wailing won out. They sat down for a rest break in the grass next to the brier patch.

"Listen, I want to make sure those dogs get good and confused. You rest here for a few minutes while I make a fake trail for them to follow," he said to Emmitt.

Emmitt said, "Yeah," and hung his head over his arms propped on his knees, fairly oblivious to everything.

Clyde hiked up the hill through the forest for a few minutes, then backtracked down to where Emmitt was now lying in the grass sound asleep.

"Come on, Emmitt! Let's go!" he said, angrily shaking him by the shoulder.

Chapter 3: The Virgin's Travels

Emmitt managed to get up and follow Clyde back into the nasty brier pit, moaning as he went.

At some point, they realized that morning had snuck up on them. The thin early light was making its way into the brier patch, starting to brighten their way. They had made it through the long night with no sleep and hardly any rest. The power-line turned down a final steep rocky drop to an open area with a large abandoned coal mine and an old prison camp and guard shack. They flopped on the ground there, exhausted.

THAT was the place where Emmitt had finally given up completely, and was soon captured and tortured by the two cruel patrolling guards, the Hicks' brothers.

Now Clyde was continuing on alone, worn out, but still determined. He stayed off the coal hauling road, back in the woods. But when the road he was running above joined a wider, more travelled road, he stopped. He recognized it as a work detail road that he had been on many times before. It was used by prison work crews out cutting trees for firewood or loading flat rocks into trucks. He knew it would be heavily patrolled, and he should avoid it.

Immediately before the junction between the two roads, there was a switchback where the coal hauling road made a bend. He retreated to the point of this switchback, and noticed concrete blocks stacked up below the road. He was curious and climbed down to investigate. He had never noticed them before, and decided they were the foundation of an old building of some sort. He decided to relieve himself, so he did so there at the edge of a patch of thorny vines, wondering what was on the other side of the tangled vegetation. He zipped up his pants, and pushed his way through the thorny undergrowth, mindlessly adding to the bleeding claw marks on his arms. On the other side he thought he could see a barely used pathway, probably mostly frequented by deer. It wandered off down the mountain, through thigh-high grass and shrubbery. He quickly decided to go that way, for lack of a better trail. He ran right through the tall grass, and kept on running until the hill fell more rapidly.

The morning light was beaming through the canopy in soft ribbons of powdery light. He wished he could climb one of those sunbeams up and out of the forest, and become a particle of light, fugitive-man no more.

He was enveloped suddenly in the midst of a pungent odor, and gave a wide berth to a dead animal of some sort, rotting in a disgusting heap by the pathway.

"Smells like shit," he mumbled. He pinched his nose shut with his thumb and forefinger and hurried past it. The smell stuck to him like grease, though.

24

Chapter 3: The Virgin's Travels

Down a steep, rocky, leg-breaking creek bed, and he suddenly found himself right above the highway. He heard voices coming from the road, and found a place where he could see from behind a tree. There were cop cars strewn across the road in a roughly fashioned blockade, with lights flashing on top, and men talking loudly. He listened but could not make out their words. He meant to cross that road somehow and find the river, but there was no chance he could do so in the vicinity of so many people.

He would have to make his way through the woods until he came to a place where he could pass over the road unobserved. He walked under cover of the forest to the left of the roadblock for three hundred feet or so. The road curved around to the right, and he could no longer see the group of men and cars. Perfect.

He kept low in the grass and weeds, and looked up and down the road. Nothing in sight, but someone might be posted in the woods with a rifle, watching. He waited for a few minutes, saw no movement, and made an instant decision to dash across the road, keeping low, arms dangling at his sides, just in case someone was watching. He threw himself over the other side and down the embankment. He lay there in the weeds, hardly breathing, listening. Had he made it? Seemed like it.

The weeds around his face drifted in a scraggly fashion upwards to catch the light. There were pretty blue flowers waving in the breeze, and some taller plants with nodding white flower clusters that reminded him of lacy women's caps. Bees were buzzing and circling over the flowers with their little feet dangling, ready for a landing. Didn't they have these types of flowers back home? Seeing them made him feel kind of homesick.

He discovered random piles of garbage amidst the weeds, and picked out a wadded up McDonalds' bag. His stomach rumbled. Maybe it had something to eat left inside. He opened it carefully, so it wouldn't rustle too much, and sure enough, there were some cold, greasy French fries inside. They tasted like salty cardboard, but he was ravenous and determined to eat them anyway. He tried to imagine them fresh and hot out of the fryer, melting on his tongue, but they made a lump like glue clogging his throat, absorbing all of his saliva, and he couldn't swallow any more.

Looking around further at the garbage strewn over the hillside, his eyes opened wide when he saw a plastic six pack holder with an unopened beer can still attached. It was his lucky day! He was going to have his first beer right here by the highway. He picked it up and twisted the beer out of its plastic necklace. He popped the top and slugged the warm, foamy liquid down his throat. At last he could swallow the bolus of French fries stuck in his throat. Three big swallows and the beer can was empty. He had hardly even tasted it.

Chapter 3: The Virgin's Travels

He felt giddy and exultant. What a great day to be alive! French fries and beer! Yeah!

The warm beer drunk so quickly made him feel light-headed and a little bit intoxicated. He rolled down the rest of the embankment, and struggled to stand up and get moving. He wandered into the woods, and began singing words to a song he made up as he went.

"I'm free, free as an eagle, flying up high....up in the sky, yeah, yeah, yeah..."

Chapter 4: The Veteran and the Vulture Tree

Friday night, Sat. morning

The fugitives seemed to have lost their way in the dark rather quickly. John had climbed to the head of the creek that flowed to the prison, seen signs that they had continued on up, and kept following them. They had bypassed the first coal mine completely, but stopped at the second one to rest a spell. He saw butt cheek imprints where they had sat next to each other in the leaves, and spots of blood on some of the leaves. Then they had apparently started wandering up and down the mountain aimlessly, probably confused and exhausted.

John knew he had crossed the boundary into the State natural area when he ran into one of its many candyass trails, kept cleared off by the prisoners for the tourist-types out seeking a pretty vista. He stood there for a moment and smoked a cigarette, enjoying the cool night air. He was startled by a small beam of light jiggling along the trail, and immediately pulled his gun out of its holster.

"Halt!" he ordered, pointing his gun at a skinny man dressed only in brief yellow nylon shorts and a white singlet, carrying a flashlight.

The man threw his hands up in the air, blinding John with the beam of light in the process, and exclaimed, "Don't shoot!"

Chapter 4: The Veteran and the Vulture Tree

John dropped his gun so the muzzle was pointing at the ground instead of the man, blinked his eyes rapidly, and said, "What the hell are you doing out here?"

The man said, "I'm just out here doing my night training. Sorry to bother you, Officer."

"Don't you know we've got a man-hunt going on?"

"Heard it on the radio, but I had to get my run in."

John had seen these types of people running on the trails recently in their skimpy outfits. He didn't know why, but they usually carried nothing but a water bottle with them, and the skinny man was no exception. He had a belt-like contraption around his waist that held two water bottles. John could see no sign of any food, emergency gear, or weapon. His shoes were flimsy nylon things with rubber soles.

"Seen anybody else out here tonight?" asked John.

"Not a soul. But listen, is it okay if I go? I'm on an eight minute per mile pace, and I'm not even tired. I've got ten more miles to go, and if I keep up the pace, I'll beat my time from last week. I've gained a total of 6,350 feet elevation so far!"

John ordered the fellow to head on down the mountain and drive back to town. He shouldn't be out there during the man-hunt. John thought he was crazy or stupid, or both, to be out in the elements practically naked like that, with no supplies. The weather could change at any moment, or he could get lost or snakebit. Or an escaped con could grab him and hold him hostage. These runner-types were obviously idiots.

John yanked on the straps of his pack, settling it on his back more firmly. He thought of all the supplies in the pack, and felt certain he could survive through any emergency situation. He watched the runner obediently sprint off down the trail towards the ranger station.

The fugitives must have given up on climbing the mountain before they reached the trail system, and descended again. He found signs that they had turned east on an old coal hauling road. But they must have been attracted to the opening made by the power-line that went up to the fire tower at the top of the mountain. They had moved over to it and inexplicably reversed direction and started down the power-line cut.

The trail led right into a hellhole of sawbriers. It was a good thing he hadn't brought the dogs. He loved his dogs, and wasn't about to let them get all cut up. Plus, the leashes would get all tangled and he would have had one heck of a time getting them back out of there.

"What a good idea," he said to himself, wryly. These men were smarter than he thought, and tougher. The briers grew over the entire hillside, roving over the power-line cut straight down the mountain. You either had to go through it or around it, or over it if you were a bird. He wished he was. But no, he would try to travel next to it, keeping it in sight, and hope that the cons had continued downhill.

John was on the look-out for a certain tree, an enormous beech tree, with branches that arched upwards like muscular arms reaching for the sky. It was the Vulture Tree.

Then he spotted it, and them. They sat high up in the branches, wings outstretched to dry their feathers, like clots of black blood blotting out the sky. This particular tree was one of their favorite roosts. Today there must have been thirty or forty of them up in its branches. The ground beneath it was littered with their white droppings. The local folks had a superstition about vulture trees. They predicted that if you walked beneath one, you were destined to die a horrible death.

"What a bunch of bull-crap," he thought, and headed away from the power-line cut, straight for the tree. He stubbornly walked beneath the roosting tree, and the noise he made caused the vultures to stir, and several lifted off the branches and beat their heavy wings to take flight away from the intruder. He knew they would circle right back and roost again.

The Virgin and The Veteran

He began going down the steep hill right next to the power-line cut, away from the briers, carefully avoiding the stubs where trees had been cut. On part of it, the cant of the hill was so steep that he had to grab roots and tree trunks to keep from falling straight down the mountain. He had to slide down parts of it on his butt, using his hands and feet to stop his momentum.

He had been all around these hills and hollers since his boyhood days of hunting coons, but he had never once been on this power-line cut, or even had the desire to climb it. It looked like a place of sorrow and pain. He continued down the side of the power-line cut, through the forest, following his notion that the escapees had gone downhill through the briers as a diversion. He expected that they had torn themselves up pretty good in the process.

A patch of grass was knocked down as if someone had taken a nap, so he figured they had come out of the briers there. Some more splatters of blood caught his eye, and he bent down to look at it, saying with certainty to himself, "Shot in the calf."

There were indications of two trails diverging there, and he stopped and circled around, confused momentarily. There were broken vines below him as if someone had gone back into the tunnel of briers, but there was also a pathway beat down in the tall grass as if someone had travelled back up the mountain. This proved what he had thought all along, that there were two fugitives travelling together. Now they had split up, but he decided that it was a temporary diversion and they would reunite soon. After whacking their way through the sawbrier jungle, he thought that they would be tired and hurting, so they probably would be going downhill. He had a hunch that the uphill trail was the false trail, and followed the downhill trail instead.

When he reached the bottom of the hill, he found himself at the old abandoned camp for prison coal miners. This was very close to the head of the creek where he had earlier continued up the mountain. If only he had searched about a little bit more in this area for signs of the convicts, he could have saved himself the trouble of climbing the mountain.

The old guard shack was still standing, and the barbed wire fence imprisoning it remained, but had places where the wire was pulled up and apart by determined vandals wanting to see inside. The quarters where the prisoners spent the night were pitifully cruel. After the back-breaking labor of hitting coal with pick axes all day, they were marched back to the camp in chains, and then had to enter their low-ceilinged abode. They could not stand up straight inside, but had to move about crouched over like gorillas.

"Pain heaped upon pain," thought John. Then, "To those who have much, much is given," he murmured out loud. It seemed to him that the Bible had so many applicable quotes to prison life, especially when it was misconstrued.

He looked around the encampment and saw where the leaves had been flattened by two bodies. Clyde and Emmitt must have rested here. There was a lot of wet blood on the leaves, so he deduced they were bleeding from their excursion through the sawbriers, in addition to the leg wound. But there were also signs of a scuffle, with the dirt all torn up around the resting place, and it looked like a body had been dragged to the road, so maybe the blood was from a fight. He found two sets of footprints in the dirt from prison-issue boots, so he suspected that two guards had captured at least one of the cons here.

He circled the leaves in a concentric fashion, bending over to study the ground for clues. There. He saw where the tall grass was bent two feet from the spot, and came upon a chewed up cud of grass. Two more feet to the dirt road, and he saw another footprint imprinted in the compacted dirt. Now he had a direction for the other convict. He had definitely headed down the coal hauling road towards the main road that led to the gap, the same way the other convict had been initially dragged.

He did not figure this convict to be a fool, not after the evasionary tactics through the sawbriers, and then escaping capture. Except for the occasional signs of passage, he had not made many mistakes. Therefore, he did not think he had stayed on the road because there would be too many guards and reporters about looking for him. John walked down the road slowly, searching along each side for clues, and searching the roadbed for more footprints. To his left there was a trail of disturbed leaves leading to a huge rocky outcropping. Above it, the trail led through the forest and then back down to the road. So this prisoner had probably hidden behind the rocks to watch the other prisoner's capture and beating, and then thought it safe to head back down to the road.

Before the coal hauling road reached the main road that led to the gap, there would be an even older trail that cut to the right off the point of a switchback and led downhill parallel to the road to the gap. John used it frequently on his dog training runs. He knew the older trail had been used as a shortcut back to the prison for many years by coal mining convicts and the guards who watched over them.

He had learned the horrible history of the unfortunate convict laborers when he was a youngster in grammar school. The convicts had been used as free labor to mine the coal in the mountains and uplift the State's economy after the Civil War. The conditions of the mines were terribly unsafe, and convicts died frequently. When one convict died, it was easy to send another to replace him.

John proudly remembered that the locals, including his grandpa's two brothers, had started a war because the Governor wouldn't listen to their pleas about the unsafe conditions in the mines. The use of free convict labor was taking away their jobs, too. The Governor sent the militia in to settle down the enraged locals, but they could not be suppressed. Over and over again, the militiamen and convict laborers were captured by the stubborn locals and put on the train back to the city. This went on for over a year, until a newly-elected Governor decided the battle could not be won against the feisty backwoods men. He abolished convict labor in the mines, but rather than losing the profits from this system entirely, he made the convicts build their own prison and coal mine. They had to mine the coal in the mountains around their stone fortress and process it themselves. This was exactly the same prison that John worked in now, every convict-laid stone still in place some eighty years later, although coal mining by prisoners had finally been abandoned.

Ahead of him beside the road he saw three men. Two were standing and one was talking on a hand-held radio in short bursts of angry conversation. The other was lying in the grass, moaning.

John walked closer, recognizing Emmitt and the Hicks' brothers.

Bubba Hicks said, "Hey, Lieutenant! Lookie what we found. Didn't need your dogs to do it neither!"

Chapter 4: The Veteran and the Vulture Tree

John just said, "Mmmm hmmmm." He didn't like the Hicks' brothers' cruel tactics and noisy ways, and normally avoided them.

"He wouldn't tell us where Clyde went, but you can try to get it out of him. We caught him up there by the old guard shack," said Bubba, the younger of the two.

Bud Hicks concluded his attempted conversation on the radio, saying, "This thing never works right out here. Can't even get through to tell them our news. Clyde can't be far away, Lieutenant. We'll take this one back and then come and help you round him up."

"No, I've got him. You all go on," John ordered quietly but sternly.

The Hicks' brothers didn't like John either, but he had earned their grudging respect in these matters, and John was their superior officer. Besides, they were ready to go off-duty and get home to their cold beers.

John observed that Emmitt looked to be a sorry mess, with torn and bloody clothing, and blood seeping out the corner of his mouth. The Hicks' brothers yanked him up on a dog leash, and he staggered along like he was about to fall with every step. He promptly collapsed on his knees on the road with his cuffed hands before him, and Bubba kicked him in the butt to make him get up again. John figured correctly that being shot and then lost for hours out in the mountains had only been part of the torture this prisoner had endured.

He nodded towards Emmitt, and told Bud, "Better clean up his face some. The highway is likely to be overrun with reporters."

He marched on past the pitiful prisoner and out about his business. There was nothing he could do. There would be more torture when he got back to the prison. It was just how things were done.

Chapter 5: The Virgin's Trials

Saturday afternoon

Clyde realized how painfully hungry he was. The beer and French fries had just primed the pump, and the heady effects of the warm beer had almost worn off. He felt in his front jeans pocket for the packet he had secreted there when he knew he was going to make a break. There it was at the bottom of his pocket, and he pulled it out. He slowed his pace, and opened the greasy brown paper wrapping. Inside was a treasure—a grilled chicken quarter! He had meant to share it with poor Emmitt, but now it was all his.

He gripped the chicken in his left hand and munched on it while he walked. He thought that a chicken quarter was a wonderfully convenient way to cut up a chicken. It left the leg and the thigh connected, so he had a nice hunk of juicy, dark chicken meat all in one package. He thought it was possibly the best thing he had ever eaten. It had a cold, greasy texture that made him smack his lips to get every drop of fat. He wished he had some baked beans to go with it.

He heard a car back on the highway that he had just crossed. He had earlier thought about trying to flag one down to steal, but had decided he didn't want to risk recapture so soon.

He felt happy eating his stolen chicken. There had been water to drink occasionally at creek crossings and sometimes muddy puddles, and the one warm beer and cold fries, but no real food until now. He had been in too much of a fever to hide and run to think about eating.

When he was finished, he licked his fingers clean, and wiped his mouth on his shirt sleeve at his armpit, in the process smelling how odorous he had become. Then he put the bones inside the brown paper, and wrapped the paper around them, sticking it back in his pocket. Maybe the dogs wouldn't smell it, he lied to himself.

He had to get going—he had been taking it easy for too long. He consulted his map, a composite of several maps drawn by prisoners who had been out on work details around the prison. "Looks like the river is near this highway somewhere down there, if I'm seeing right." Maybe if he just headed downhill he would run into it. So he started through the underbrush downhill and tried to keep a straight course. At a fifty-gallon drum, just beginning to show signs of rust, he headed left, continuing downhill.

The sky had been looking ominously gray all afternoon, and he was half-worried it would rain. The other half of him was hoping for a cool shower to cut the heat of the day. Sure enough, rain started spattering on his arms, then the sky unloaded a raging river of water down on him. Soon he was drenched to the skin, and feeling morose.

He started singing a made-up song in a low voice, as he trudged through the cold rain. Singing was what he often did to pass the time.

"I was shakin' in my boots,
just shakin' in my boots,
When I saw my Lord nailed upon that tree!
Ooooh, just shakin' in my boots."

When he sang the words, "shakin' in my boots," indeed, he was shaking. But it wasn't due to religious fervor—it was more due to the cold and the gnawing fear that he felt. He didn't even consider himself to be religious at all, but had grown up in the south and attended the local Baptist church sporadically. The old hymns had been forgotten, except for an occasional phrase or two.

Shivering and wet, he remembered the "Bad Thing" that the other prisoners said lived out here in the woods. It had assumed mythological proportions, until most of the old timers spoke of it in hushed tones. The Bad Thing was supposed to come out in the forest around the prison and hunt people down and tear them apart, the same way he had torn apart the chicken quarter. It even ate its young. The Bad Thing ate its victims—leg, thigh, butt, arm—piece by piece while they were still alive and screaming. Clyde had heard the tale so often that he usually shrugged it off as one more stupid prison story. But now, under his new circumstances, he was scared. Bad Thing or not, he was feeling awfully sick of the whole ordeal.

He crossed an old jeep road and thought about taking it, but then he saw a sheer rock wall ahead of him, running above a creek. He decided to walk on the trail above it upstream for a ways, thinking the bluffs were never going to end, but gradually the rock face changed. Jumbles of huge rocks appeared, as if giants had used enormous sledgehammers on the cliff and broken the rocks up.

He was weary, wet, and hungry. The rain was interminable, and he felt like a wet rabbit seeking cover. He needed to find a place to hide and rest until the rain let up, and hoped there might be a cave somewhere in the rocks, or at least a little hidden place tucked away, so he searched avidly, looking left and right, high and low, trying to see.

At last, he saw a rock ledge jutting out to his right, down about six feet. Maybe it sheltered an opening or a cave. He hopped down the rocks to see.

He got to the ledge and dropped in front of it, and crouched to look inside. It appeared to be perfect. It was just an indentation from the rest of the rocks, into the mountain about four feet. No bears or panthers jumped out at him. He bent over and scooted under the ledge and felt along the rough back wall for further indentations. There were none. The floor was loose dirt, dry in the furthest part of the recess, and moist from the rain near the opening. He immediately sat down with his back to the rock and pulled his knees up to his chest and sighed.

He wanted to take a little nap, just a short one. Maybe he had fooled the dog trackers into thinking he went on upstream where he had waded in the water. If only he could doze off quickly, and wake up in just 20 minutes, and get on his way, he thought he would be safe. He rolled over onto his side, legs still tucked up, head resting on his left arm. He looked out into the rain-drenched world and imagined the Bad Thing coming for him and finding him and tearing into his flesh. It was hard to sleep with the specter of that image hovering over him. He imagined the Bad Thing as a huge, hairy beast with enormous teeth, lunging and growling and biting.

His thoughts roamed to something else. He started reflecting upon his past deeds. Why did he always end up back in prison? He couldn't seem to break out of the rut. At first, he had just stolen money as a fun thing to do. But then he had gotten older and needed money to live on, to buy food, pay rent, and buy cheap whiskey. He couldn't hold down a job because he was always on the run evading the law. And he felt like all those stupid law-abiding people were in his way, and it wasn't fair that they had money and he didn't. So he robbed them and paid for his needs. He deserved it. What else was he going to do? He couldn't live the way they did—he had to have his freedom. Whenever he got caught by the law, they threw him back in prison. He would try and try to escape every time. Usually he ended up paying for it with more time behind bars. Whenever they finally let him back out, they still told him what to do, where to be, and how to live his life. He hated it. He wanted his freedom, and that meant being able to do what he wanted and when he wanted. He didn't want to work at some grocery sacking up canned goods for old ladies, and living hand to mouth on the few dollars they threw at him, towing the line to be "reformed". He might as well be in prison, if he had to live the life they insisted he live on the outside. His only choice was to continue to seek his freedom, whether it was inside the prison wall or outside. Inside, he tried to get out. Outside, he tried to have his way, and ended up getting thrown back in. It was a vicious circle. For as long as he remembered, it had been that way.

This time around, they had thrown the book at him and given him life in prison. They told him he was a killer, but he had never killed anyone in his whole life! The things he did wrong that landed him behind bars were generally just to get money to live on. He didn't have it in him to kill anyone, he was pretty sure.

He was petrified by the thought of being electrocuted. Sit in a chair and have your flesh fried while you were still alive? Have your hair burst into flames while your hands were manacled to a chair? Have your eyeballs melt and run down your face into your screaming mouth?

Chapter 5: The Virgin's Trials

He was incarcerated in a prison where all the murderers and violent criminals were sent, deep in the backwoods of the south, surrounded by tall mountains, wild animals, and stalwart local hillbillies who would just as soon shoot you as talk to you.

In the midst of all the reminiscing about the past, the pull of sleep became irresistible, even though he was cold and wet, and so hungry that his stomach hurt. He dozed off into the land of dreams, rubbing his growling stomach into submission.

He tossed fitfully in his wet clothing on the hard ground. He managed to sleep, but it was not a good sleep or a deep one. The Man came to him in his dreams.

The Man stood before him, and Clyde hunkered down at the rear of the overhang, trembling in fear. The Man was bent down, peering at him under the ledge, saying, "What are you doing in there?"

Clyde was too scared to answer, and his teeth chattered. The Man had a sadistic, leering grin. "Shit-eating grin" was what Clyde's father would have called it. He had on a long, worn-out leather duster that reached to mid-calf, and was stiff and stained from lack of care. It was unbuttoned and Clyde could see the Man had on blue jeans and old boots. He had a gut breaking out over his belt. His leather hat flopped over his ears, and his huge eyes bugged out of his face and bore holes into Clyde's soul.

"What are you, a Quitter? A Wimp? A Weenie? If you sit in here, you'll never make it. They'll roast you alive when they catch you!" The Man said in an all-knowing voice. "These woods are no place for Losers. You are a Loser, aren't you?"

The Man was holding something out towards Clyde, almost within his reach. It was a chunk of something that was smeared with dark red sauce and was dripping blood. Chicken, he immediately knew it was chicken. He reached out his hand impulsively, unthinkingly, wanting it worse than anything.

The Man said, "Yes, chicken for Quitters. Go on, take it. Then sit there and die." He extended his arm and the chicken was almost in Clyde's grasp.

But then, Clyde's shoulders slumped, and he dropped his hand to the dirt floor. He didn't want chicken. More than anything he wanted his freedom. The chicken could wait.

The Man backed away from the opening, turned and walked away, tearing into the bloody chicken himself, and muttering with his mouth full, "Heh, heh, heh."

Clyde jolted awake then, and looked about, startled. Where was he? He got on his hands and knees and looked tentatively out from under the ledge. No sign of The Man. But he had seemed so real, and the chicken…he could almost taste the cloying sweetness of the sauce, and feel the chewy raw flesh of the chicken on his tongue.

Exasperated and hungry, he came out from under the ledge, and stood up and stretched. It was time to move on into the valley and let the phantoms of the mountain haunt each other instead of him.

The rain had finally stopped, and he looked up for a moment out of his moroseness, and felt hope again. The sky had cleared up some, and the sun was coming out. He could see the wet branches of the trees glistening in the sunlight.

But his hopes were dashed when the fog started filling up the forest with a ghost-like speed to take its turn torturing him. Soon he couldn't even see his hand before his face.

He followed the bluff above the creek upstream for a ways, and found a place where water drained down the rocks from above into the creek. He decided to climb down the wash, but was in too much of a hurry, and lost his balance. He tumbled down through the rocks, bashing his knees and hips, and landed in a heap at the base of the cliff.

"Ouch!" he muttered. "Dumb ass!" He stood up and rubbed his hips and knees to see if they were broken. Satisfied that they were merely bruised, he tried to look around through the fog. He could barely see the creek ahead and stumbled to it, and rushed across it, not even attempting to rock hop.

He wandered here and there, from rock to rock and tree to tree, loping along in a disorganized fashion, fighting with himself about his fears, and not paying attention to where he was physically any more.

The grim and frightened voice in his head kept telling him things like "You're never going to get out of these woods alive!" "You're never going to have freedom again!" "You're never going to make it!"

"Damn!" he exclaimed as he suddenly ran right into a tree, and fell down into the mud.

He felt like curling up into a little ball and waiting right there until morning. But he didn't. He was too chilled from his wet clothing and had to keep moving. There was a loud, rushing noise before him, like falling water. His feet hit a solid sheet of rock, and he took one more step onto the rock, and then one more, and then there was no more rock to walk on. Just empty space. He pulled his foot back to the rock hastily, and grabbed blindly for something to hold onto, luckily grasping a tree limb to help him keep his balance.

"Ho!" he cried out. He wondered how far a drop was in front of him. Maybe it was a cliff over a waterfall? He didn't know exactly what it was and didn't want to find out. So he backed off the rock, and decided not to walk on any more rocks, but to keep his feet on the ground. He continued his random wandering around with his arms outstretched like a blind person, bumping into every tree and rock.

It reminded him of "Blind Man's Bluff", the game he and the neighborhood kids had played in the streets where he grew up. All the kids stood in a circle, and the "blind" man was blindfolded with an old bandana and spun around in the center. He twirled around the circle of kids and tried to grab them. Everyone screamed and jumped away from you, but you had to grab someone in order to win your freedom. The way to win was to listen to the sounds of breathing or movement they made and estimate where they were standing, then suddenly jump at them and grab them.

Was there anything to hear out here? He stopped in his tracks and listened. Nothing but his own frantically beating heart and panicked breathing. But then, there was a crack off to his left, like a branch breaking. He held his breath and froze where he was. "Who's there???" he said in a shaky voice.

There was no answer.

Then he heard a deep, coughing noise, even closer. Was it some animal tracking him in the fog by the chicken smell in his pocket? Or was it one of the guards coming after him?

His nerves were shooting fire up and down his legs and arms, and his breathing was coming in short bursts. Was it the Bad Thing, coming to get him and devour him? He traversed the hillside by slamming into trees, falling down, and jumping back up, over and over.

"Just keep going," he lectured himself. "Just keep going." Finally he collapsed from lack of air and lay on the wet ground whimpering and shaking. Was it coming? It was a few minutes before he was able to hold his breath and listen. Nothing. For long moments he heard nothing. He began to breathe again, semi-relaxing, letting the fear run out of him onto the ground in the form of hot urine, soaking the front of his pants.

He started talking to himself out loud, a habit he had gotten into when alone. "Come on, you dumb ass, there's nothing out there. You can do this. Don't lose it. Things could get a lot worse. Think about going back to solitary in that stupid Hole back there. They'll leave you in there to rot. You've got to keep going, no matter what."

He was miserably ashamed about wetting his pants, but he couldn't help it. He guessed the piss-smell would just blend in with all the other nasty smells he had accumulated in the last two days.

He thought about prison life while he lay there. When he was in prison, he was a model prisoner except for one thing. He never stopped thinking about escaping, and trying to escape. It was something he could not control, like an involuntary muscle twitch. He had tried to escape every which way he could think of, and only succeeded once from another prison, and then only briefly. It had gotten to be a challenge, sort of a game that he played. He'd show them how it was done! And he had. Here he was, out of there, free. But what a lousy freedom it was—rain, fog, cliffs, imaginary monsters, snakes, bears, people and dogs hunting you down, all alone, scared, exhausted, hurting all over, and even peeing on yourself.

To top it all off, he urgently needed to have a bowel movement. The greasy chicken and then the flight through the forest after drinking the beer must have cranked up his digestive system. He walked into some dark green bushy plants and lowered his wet pants. His legs were shivering while he squatted, and the pesky gnats and mosquitoes were having a heyday with his butt cheeks. The wet leaves would have to suffice for wiping himself somewhat clean. Then he pulled his pants back up, still feeling miserably glum.

The fog was lifting, and Clyde could finally see the creek below him. He backtracked down from the hill to the creek and shuffled through the water a ways.

"Mess up my scent," he thought.

The riffles swirled and splashed, and the pools fled from his feet as if in sudden surprise. He debated with himself whether to continue trekking up the hill to see what was up there. He was overwhelmingly tired and depressed.

Why should he go on? Why not just give up? Head up the hill to the road and flag down a car and turn himself in. He entertained this idea for a few minutes, then shook his head vehemently back and forth.

What the hell! He had come this far. He jutted out his chin and nodded his head.

"Cut the bullshit and get your ass in gear." That's what his Pa had always said, usually with his boot kicking Clyde's butt. So he started walking uphill again, pushing himself to finish the race he had begun.

Chapter 6: The Veteran in the Fog

Saturday afternoon

John found very few signs of passage. Except for a few more boot prints, there was nothing of interest. When he came to where he knew the old shortcut trail branched off, he stopped to seek more signs. The entrance to the old trail had grown up into weeds and a thicket of thorny vines, bursting with hard, red, unripe blackberries. A few more weeks and he would be having a feast right there. He noticed where the underbrush had been pushed back to allow an opening for someone. He went that way too, and stepped over and through the thorny vines, pulling them away from his face and arms as best he could. They raked his legs like cat claws, but did not break through his tough work jeans.

He could barely make out the pathway headed downhill. The blackberry thicket gave way, and he only had to deal with tall grass and knee high bushes and small trees. He knew there were likely to be numerous seed ticks in the tall grass, just waiting for a blood meal, so he avoided walking in it.

He wasn't surprised to feel droplets of water splashing on his hands, as it often rained in the summer afternoons. He looked up, out from under his hat brim, and saw rain splashing on the oak leaves and dripping down onto him. One drop splashed right into his eye, and he closed it reflexively and ducked his head under his hat. The rain drops began coming down faster and soon he would be in a downpour.

Luckily, he always carried a poncho in his small pack. He unzipped the brown canvas pack, pulled out the bright orange plastic sheet and tucked his body into it hastily.

One never knew what the weather would do in these mountains. He was always prepared for any event, with a space blanket for warmth, beef jerky and chocolate bars for nutrients, water for thirst, and a map and compass (although truth be told, he really didn't know how to use the compass, and the mental map in his head was all he ever needed.)

He remembered a different man-hunt one spring when the rainy weather suddenly broke down into flooding, and the gullies and creeks had erupted into white rushing spigots. Sheets of water had washed down the steep hills, and everything had turned to mush. That time the escaped prisoner had found himself surrounded on a little island of land by the rising waters and was terrified, and the guards had easily corralled him and hauled him through the water and back to the prison.

The rain was coming down thickly. Without his poncho, he would be soaked to the skin in minutes. He continued on down the old road, but his legs and feet were soon ensconced in thick clinging jeans and wet leather. The water ran down the poncho and soaked his pant legs and then drained into his boots. He wondered how Clyde was faring ahead of him, with no rain cover at all. But then, maybe he had found an overhang of rock to sit under and wait for the rain to dispense.

The rain shower petered out into splashes and sputters, then suddenly stopped as immediately as it had begun. John shook out the poncho but kept it on for a bit so it would dry. Nothing he could do about his wet pants and boots, so he squished on down the hill. Guards were used to adversity, and learned to shoulder on.

He thought about how he had come to be a prison guard, back in the beginning of his thoughts about prison life. As a young boy, he had spent his free time circling the prison out in the woods, hunting and fishing. He knew the prison's footprint on everyone's life in the area. It WAS their life. Everyone's daddy worked there, and everyone's momma hated it.

Once he got out of high school, he knew his destiny. His momma knew it too, but it made her cry. She begged his daddy not to take John to work with him that day.

"It's time. He's a man now. Let's go, John," said his father.

John had obeyed his daddy and followed him to work in the prison. It was his first time through the steel gates into the mysterious domain of thugs and thieves. He had dreamed so many nightmares about being there, and was afraid.

"You stay with me for a while," his daddy said.

John stuck to his father like a leech. They entered the prison doors, and they clanged behind him noisily. This made him jump and look back. The doors were closed and he was on the inside, unable to get back out. His heart was thumping crazily in his chest. He wanted back out badly.

"Come on," his father said. "We've got to get you a uniform and a badge. Then we'll start making the rounds."

Once John was dressed up in guard gear and badge, he was issued a revolver, which he turned over and over in his hands, memorizing its every detail. Then he holstered it. He didn't need to be trained in its use, or pass any shooting skills exams. He had been born to use it. He could shoot a squirrel between the eyes from fifty paces, easy.

He followed his father around the prison all day, and the convicts looked him up and down.

"Pretty boy, ain't you?" said one old geezer, licking his lips.

Others on his cellblock picked up the term, and he heard, "Pretty boy!" and cat calls and whistles all

Chapter 6: The Veteran in the Fog

morning. His dad told them to shut up, and then told John to ignore it, that it would change to something worse by tomorrow.

By the end of the morning, he was pretty sick of the "Pretty boy" thing, and about to let go of his temper and maybe even use his gun. His dad knew it, too.

"Look, John, these guys are going to try to get at you however they can. They know you're new at this, and wet behind the ears. Don't let them see how pissed you are. Just take it in stride, and go on and do your job. This too shall pass," his dad said, quoting the Bible like he did every day for everything.

At that time in his life, John had liked the Bible verse, "An eye for an eye, a tooth for a tooth." He had fought his way through high school, and had earned the local boys' respect. He figured he would have to start over in here. The next creep that called him "Pretty boy" was going to rue the day.

As they rounded the corner into the next cell-block, checking cells and counting men, the first guy they came to was clutching the bars to his cell, and glaring at the guards. He spit at their feet, and whined, "I hear you got a Pretty boy, there, Lieutenant Rankin."

John reached through the bars and grabbed the thug by the neck with both hands, before he could even wink. He held on, squeezing. The criminal let go of the bars and raised his hands up to try to pry John off his throat, gasping for air, and crying out.

"John! Let go!" his father commanded.

"No!" John growled back, squeezing harder. But his father ruled, and John knew he had to let go. But just for a moment, he kept a hold of the guy, shaking him.

"Call me Pretty again, and I'll kill you. I'll kill all of you," He said through clenched teeth. Then he let go, and pushed the feller backwards.

The convict stumbled, holding his throat and rubbing. "You're crazy, boy, durn crazy. You're gonna end up locked in here too. Cause you belong in here, you know you do!"

John took that in and let it sink to his stomach, where it digested for quite some time. But none of the convicts ever called him "Pretty boy" again. His father was proud of him, but never told him.

John stopped dreaming about the past when he walked into a wall of fog. Fog whooshed up out of the valley all around him, stroking him and whispering to him. Fog was funny in these parts. You came upon it suddenly, and it rose up to meet you. You could either sit tight for a while or keep going through it to the other side. It was a cloud of moisture hugging the earth, where hot and cold air had met and become one. He could not see a foot in

Chapter 6: The Veteran in the Fog

front of him. He didn't want to retreat back up the hill, because that would take up too much of his energy. If he kept going, he might end up wandering off the road and have to figure out where he was later. It was time for a rest, anyway.

The best thing he could do was hunker down and wait it out. He had found that to be the case with most of life's adversities, including the bad weather in these mountains. So he sat down with his back to a ramrod straight tulip poplar, wrapped the wet poncho about him, and pulled out a cigarette. It was a bad habit, but he had quit caring. Something was going to kill him anyway—might as well enjoy the process. He inhaled deeply, and the nicotine relaxed him. When he was done, he twisted the butt into the mud next to him to put it out, then pocketed it. He didn't like leaving garbage in the woods.

Finally, he pulled his hat down over his eyes and closed them. He would let the fog explore the mountain side while he enjoyed a little shuteye. He drifted off to sleep instantly, but he napped in an aware state, like a mountain lion, and could be awake and in action mode in two seconds at any noise.

After a while, he was startled awake by a cracking sound. It was close by, and he heard it again, coming towards him. What was it? He imagined it might be a panther. He had heard tales of panther sightings all his life, but never seen sign of one.

The noises got louder. He jumped up and unholstered his gun, ready to fire into the mist.

The fog swirled about his face, and then parted momentarily. There was the form of a man approaching him, hazy and distorted.

"Who goes there?" he yelled.

"John? Is that you?"

John instantly recognized his buddy, Guard Stockstill, by his voice.

"What the hell are you doing running around in the fog, Harry?"

"Thought you might be up here goofing off," joked Harry.

They eyed each other through the clearing mist and grinned. Guard Stockstill's grin was difficult to see due to the bushy moustache covering his upper lip entirely, and trailing down to his chin.

John said, "You know I don't move around much in the fog. I was waiting it out. Looks like it's clearing up now. What's it like down there?"

Harry exploded. "Oh, the road is crawling, just crawling with FBI agents and reporters. You won't believe it. I've never seen anything like it. They think they know so much about hunting down escapees, and they're trying to tell us what to do. But we ain't gonna do what they say, no way," he said emphatically, shaking his head back and forth.

John was surprised at his friend's uncharacteristic outburst. "Yeah, they always come out here putting their noses into our business, don't they," said John dryly, remembering the last famous escaped convict they had chased down and captured. The FBI had tried to run the show then, too.

The fog had pushed on up and out of the hollow into the sunlight, and disappeared. John reholstered his gun in its shoulder holster, then tore off his poncho and attempted to fold it. "Dang nab it! I never can get these things folded right," he exclaimed as he tried to tighten it into a small package.

"Here, let me do it," said Harry.

John handed him the sloppy poncho mess, and watched him fold it meticulously and tightly into a smooth bundle. "You sure have a knack for that. Too bad you can't get a job as a poncho folder," commented John.

He stuffed it into his pack and slung it over his right shoulder, then poked his left arm through the left strap and centered the weight of it on his back with a shake.

Harry removed his own poncho, shook it, and carefully folded it into his own pack.

"The Hicks boys caught Emmitt up at the guard shack. Gave him a beating to remember, plus he's gunshot in the calf. Clyde went down this way, I'm pretty sure. Hopefully you haven't messed up his tracks too bad," said John.

"I didn't see nary a sign of him, but you're the expert," said Harry.

Wilson and Whitey suddenly appeared from behind them. They were being towed by two brown and black bloodhounds. The dogs were eager to greet John, and pulled their handlers frantically to his side. John reached down and petted their heads, while the wet dogs leaned against him.

"Good dog, Blue, Good dog, Punkin," he said. "Glad you boys finally caught up. See any sign of them?"

"We followed you up the creek bed, then well, sheeeeet, we kind of lost the scent in the woods." Wilson hung his head, embarrassed. "So we headed on back down to Coal Mine 7. Then we picked up the scent again and followed it to here."

Wilson's long hair and beard were dripping from the rain, and his clothing was soaked and ripped. John was puzzled that he wore no socks with his holey tennis shoes and asked him about it.

Chapter 6: The Veteran in the Fog

"Man, I don't even own a pair of socks," said Wilson, shrugging his shoulders apathetically. "Never saw the need for 'em."

Punkin's tongue was hanging out and she felt like she had a temperature. John realized the dogs were ready for a rest and a good long drink. It was about time for them to be traded for some fresh dogs.

They continued on down the road into a thickly forested area, and then they had to hustle down a long steep stretch. At one point, John pulled his red bandana out of his back pocket and covered his mouth and nose with it. He noticed that Harry was doing the same thing ahead of him.

"Ungulate," said Harry, glancing over his shoulder at John.

"Ungu-what?" asked John. "What the hell are you talking about?" He knew there was a dead and decaying feral hog just ahead of them. Probably been shot by a hunter who didn't catch up with it, and it came up here to die. The carcass had been there for two days. It was beginning to come alive with maggots and beetles, and the stench was awful. The coyotes had been feasting on it too.

"Hoofed mammal," said Harry, pointing his chin at the carcass.

The Virgin and The Veteran

"You read too much," said John, thinking about Harry alone in his house reading every night. His two sons were grown and worked in the prison, and his wife was gone much of the time taking care of her elderly father. Harry spent his time reading, mostly geographical magazines and science books he got from the library. John could understand the geographical magazines, with all those photos of bare-breasted native women, but the science books puzzled him. Every once in a while Harry spouted off some scientific term or weird fact, which would have been annoying coming from anybody else. At least he didn't go on and on about it, but kept it short. John had learned a few things from Harry about identifying things in the woods by their proper name and family. He didn't know how useful that was, but sometimes it was surprisingly interesting.

Wilson and Whitey were having a time of it with Blue and Punkin. The dogs were anxious to roll in the stinky carcass, and were straining forward mightily on their harnesses. The men had to yank them back from it, yelling, "No! Nooo! Leave it!"

They ran onward. Harry set a lively pace, with a quick kick to his steps. He had a lean, wiry body just made for running. John admired his friend's speed and confidence in traversing the backcountry. After a short distance, they started down a very steep creek bed which plummeted down the mountainside. It was hard to keep from tripping and falling in the rocks.

Chapter 6: The Veteran in the Fog

The creek went under the highway where two FBI agents met them at a blockade. John could see two cars with flashing lights parked by the road with dogs in the backseats, howling insanely at the sight of Punkin and Blue. There were four more agents standing in a circle, talking with arms folded over their chests. The agents were dressed in black suits, bright white dress shirts, and black ties, with shiny black dress shoes. How on earth they planned to conduct a man-hunt in the backcountry dressed like that was beyond John's imagination. There were four civilians too, and one of them was at his elbow, scribbling notes with a short pencil on a notepad. Another one was in his face, snapping the flash on his camera in his eyes and blinding him. Wilson and Whitey held their dogs firmly over at the road's shoulder, waiting for John's orders.

"What have you found out there?" demanded the slightly stout agent, with a crisp Yankee accent, pushing his small glasses back up on his wide nose.

"We caught one of them at the old coal mine," said John, blinking his eyes rapidly to be rid of the bright yellow light from the flashbulb.

The agent's radio burst into loud static, "DC, come in, DC, answer."

The agent flipped a switch and started talking into it in short stabs of code language, then broke away from the radio to tersely and conspiratorially ask John, as if they were best buddies, "Was it Clyde?"

"No, it was Emmitt Rothschild," said John.

The radio exploded again with static, "DC, come on back, DC. Stay on the line, that's an order."

The agent returned to his code talking with whoever was on the other end, then abruptly ended the conversation and asked John, "Was there more than one?"

"No, just the one," lied John. No way was he going to have these agents messing up his trail to Clyde! He was going to have to outwit them. He knew the Hicks' brothers wouldn't tell them about Clyde, either.

Again, the radio demanded the agent's attention, with its loud eruption of static, and the voice demanding, "DC, what's the deal? Stay on the line!"

The agent angrily flipped off the radio, and said, "Damn," spitting on the road. "We've got to find Clyde, and soon. Have you found any sign of him at all? We need to get our dogs on his trail, and then we'll bring him in."

"No, no sign of Clyde," lied John again. "He might have caught a ride. The locals hereabouts think he's a hero."

Chapter 6: The Veteran in the Fog

"Stupid redneck hillbillies," said the younger of the two agents, while rolling a breath mint around in his mouth.

John thought they were the stupid ones. They didn't even know that almost all of the guards were locals and proud to be hillbillies.

A helicopter whirred by overhead, passing them on its way to the prison ball field for a landing.

"Well, we've got to go report back to the prison now," John said, backing away, and he and Harry took off at a jog down the highway to the prison. Wilson and Whitey followed with the two tired and thirsty dogs.

An old rusted-out green pick-up truck came chugging down the highway from the gap. Two guards were sitting in the cab, windows down, with their elbows hanging on the sills. They waved and nodded as they slowly rolled through the group of FBI agents and reporters. It was Bubba and Bud— but where was Emmitt? They drove right by John and the other guards, holding up their hands as if to say, "No room!" and sneering. They gunned the truck as they passed them, and noxious exhaust spurted out the tailpipe.

"Assholes," Harry muttered.

As they went by, John noticed a tarp wrapped around something rather large in the back of the truck. Was it Emmitt? Hidden away from the prying eyes of the FBI?

John had it in his mind to get his two newly trained dogs and come back and start on the trail where they had left off at the road, but they would have to shortcut through the woods and pick up the scent where the FBI agents couldn't see them.

He wasn't about to let those sorry-ass agents get his man.

Chapter 7: The Virgin and the White Rock

Saturday evening

There was a bright opening ahead, where the woods ended and a grassy field began. Clyde looked up and saw a power line high overhead, the conduit for electricity to the prison and the nearby town. He turned left and headed up the power line right-of-way. After a few minutes he realized what a sitting duck he was, right out there in the open. It was too easy, so he scurried back into the woods, under cover.

His eyes were looking down at the forest floor so he would not trip, but occasionally he allowed himself stolen glances around at the forest. It was both eerie and lovely, with the trees appearing to be dark, shadowy soldiers marching in rows up the hill.

There were shiny white rocks at his feet, and he picked one up and turned it over and over in his hands. It was shot through with a pink vein, and was just the right size to hold in the palm of his hand and fold his fingers over. It was smooth and hard. He put it in his pocket for later. If it came down to being captured and thrown back in the dark Hole for days on end, he might still have this small beautiful object to look at by the light that came through the crack in the trap door. It might keep him sane. Otherwise, there was nothing in that Hole but chill grimness and darkest night.

The Virgin and The Veteran

The pretty rock reminded him of a pretty girl who had been visiting him in prison. Alice was a journalist who had been assigned to write up his story for her newspaper. She came once a week from the State capital and spent an hour asking him questions through the glass window with the little grill at the bottom in the visiting room. She was young and pretty, with short blonde hair. He had always had a thing for blondes. She wasn't like the girls he had known, though, because she was smart and very business-like. She was sitting in her chair, notebook and pen ready, when the guard brought him in. He sat down and she began shooting him questions. He always answered them, but not always truthfully. He enjoyed the attention of the media, and having his picture in the newspaper. He couldn't see why he should tell the absolute truth anyway. It was more fun to make stuff up. That way they kept sending people to talk to him, like the lovely Alice.

"So did you kill him or not?" she finally asked him one day.

"Yes, and no," he replied.

"What????" she said, exasperated with him.

"Everyone says I did, so I must have," he said.

"But did you really do it?" she asked again, brown eyes open wide and glaring holes through the glass.

Chapter 7: The Virgin and the White Rock

Her lips were pursed together in dissatisfaction at his answers.

"Sure," he said, "Why not. I must have killed him, right?" he said, being flippant with her.

"But did you pull the trigger and kill him?" she practically screamed, sitting on the edge of her seat.

The guard on duty was shifting back and forth on his feet nervously, and coughing loudly.

Clyde decided it might be time to calm Alice down.

"No, I didn't kill him. Don't you believe me?" he cocked his head, and smiled sweetly at her.

"Ooooooh!!!" She rolled her eyes and sighed. "What am I going to say in my article?"

"Just say I did it. It's easier that way."

She got up and began putting away her pen and paper into her big black purse. "I don't know if I can keep coming here to talk to you. You just talk in circles and get me so confused."

"It's kind of fun, though, isn't it?" he said, in a cheery tone, faking happiness.

"No, it makes me mad."

"Oh, I'll tell you the truth next time. I promise."

She walked towards the exit door, and the guard moved to grab Clyde's arm and take him from the room. The guard poked him hard in the side, and whispered, "Quit messing with her, asshole."

Clyde ignored him, and called out, "See you next week," looking over his shoulder as he walked to the door. Alice, beautiful Alice, she was hooked, and would be back, he just knew it.

Alice would come back every week for ten weeks, until she finally got her article written about his sorry life of crime. She was never sure whether he pulled the trigger or not, but she eventually concluded in her article that he couldn't have done it. After the article was published, she continued coming to visit him, to his delight.

Now that he was free, he thought about looking up her phone number and calling her. He knew she would read about his escape, and be very upset with him. But maybe he could get her to meet him somewhere. It would be the happiest time of his life if he could spend time with her on the outside.

There was a road ahead of him, so he slowed down and hid behind a tree to check things out. Looked to be an old jeep road. There was no one about that he could see, so he walked across it, cheerily whistling, thinking about Alice.

Chapter 8: The Veteran is Delayed

Saturday evening

"The Warden wants to see you, John," said Connelly. John and Harry and the other two men were coming through the gate with the dogs, ready to take them to the kennel.

"Can I get the dogs situated first?" asked John.

"No, you better head on up there pronto," said Connelly.

"Harry..." John began, turning to his right-hand man.

"I got it," interrupted Harry. "No prob. See ya later." Harry took both dogs off to the kennel to get them out of their harnesses and fix them some food and water. Wilson and Whitey headed to the kitchen to find some dinner.

John stoically headed to the Warden's office to see what was what in the administration world. He took off his hat on the way and put it in his pack.

The Warden's secretary greeted him and led him to the Warden's office door. When John looked in, he was surprised by the number of people in the office. Looked to be quite a party going on.

"Lieutenant Rankin, come on in. These men are from the Federal Bureau of Investigation," said the Warden. He turned to the agents and bragged, "This is Lieutenant John Rankin, our best man-hunter. Always gets his man." Then he turned back to John and said, waving his hand in the direction of a dark-haired swarthy man, "John, this is Agent Maxwell. He's the agent in charge of this investigation."

John shook hands with Agent Maxwell, and all the rest of them. The Warden motioned him to a chair. John sat down obediently.

The FBI men started firing questions at him about the escape and the ongoing man-hunt. John acted bewildered by all the questions. Agent Maxwell cut in, and drawled, "Hush you all. Let me handle this."

"Now, Looootenant, we jest wanna know what all has been goin' on out there. Can ya tell us whatcha know?" Two of the other agents were snickering behind their hands.

"Yes sir," said John, a bit confused by the FBI man's fakey backwoods accent. He was clearly a Yankee. John wondered if he wasn't making fun of him, trying to talk like a hillbilly. He gave a brief report of his activities. "I've been out all night following a track up to the old coal mines, and then circling the track round about. I ran into the Hicks brothers after they captured Emmitt. Then I met up with Guard Stockstill, Whitey and Wilson, and two of my dogs, all worn out with the hunt. We all came

Chapter 8: The Veteran is Delayed

on down the old coal mining road to the highway, and headed on back here to get some food and turn in the dogs for some fresh ones."

"So do ya know if you were followin' Clyde?" Agent Maxwell continued with his questioning.

"No sir, can't be certain," said John.

"Was Emmitt travellin' all by hisself then?" asked Maxwell.

"Unlikely, but still not sure. I need to get my fresh dogs out there right away to find out," said John.

"Excuse me, Sir, but we need him to fill out this report with his signature and give it to the secretary before he goes. Just standard procedure," interrupted a fat, bespectacled FBI agent.

"But I need to get my dogs and get going again," objected John.

"You'd better do what they say NOW, John," ordered the Warden impatiently.

"Yes sir," sighed John, wondering how long this was going to take. Paperwork was his least favorite part of the job. Seemed to take forever and be totally useless. The FBI would make it even worse with added forms to fill out and questions to answer. He longed for the old days when he simply went out and captured his man.

He exited the office and sat down by Nancy's desk, filling out the ten page form as quickly as he could. Finally he signed his name, handed her all of the papers, and strode off down the hallway. First he stopped off at the kitchen and grabbed a few bites of dinner and got something to drink, and then he went to the kennels intent upon getting Elvis and Sassy ready to go. Harry met him at the entrance with the dogs on their leashes, harnesses already on.

"They've been fed and had a drink. Blue and Punkin have bedded down for the night. Let's go," said Harry.

"Well, shit. You after my job or something?" asked John. He had halfway expected that Harry would be so efficient.

"Yeah, I'm dying to deal with those assholes up there," said Harry.

The dogs were anxious to go, jumping up on John with their tails wagging furiously. Once they had their harnesses on, they knew it was time to work, and they lived for working. They loved the hunt more than anything, even more than their dinners.

John filled his canteen and grabbed an extra supply of chocolate and beef jerky, just in case. He stuck it all in his pack quickly, and at the same time retrieved his hat and put it on. He could have used a brief rest, but he was eager to go again, too.

Chapter 8: The Veteran is Delayed

"Okay, we're off," he said to Harry. Out they went into the prison yard, hurrying by the ogling, gossiping groups of prisoners.

"Any word on Clyde?" yelled out a prisoner.

"Nope, nothing yet," said John.

"Hope the rattlesnakes get you!" shouted another prisoner.

"Go to hell," said Harry.

John and Harry exited the main gate and walked through the parking lot. John observed all the cars that normally weren't there, noticing the many out-of-state license plates. They took off down the road, tired but pumped up with the adrenaline of the hunt. It was going to be a fun night in the woods.

Chapter 9: The Virgin Meets a Foe

Saturday evening and Saturday night

"Let's all go to the river,
Then we can wash ourselves clean,
And Jesus will set us free,
Way down yonder at the river!"

Clyde sang his made-up song quietly under his breath as he hiked down the steep hill. Surely the river was just ahead!

He consulted his crudely drawn map again, digging it out of the pocket that held the pretty white rock. Unfortunately, the highway needed to be traversed again before he could get to the river and cross over it. He had planned poorly again.

When he got to the highway, he crept up to it and peered about. It was almost dark, and the full moon was rising. There were two dark cars parked in a row, blocking traffic passage on the highway completely. No people seemed to be about. But then he thought he saw movement in the car closest to him. Could the FBI agents be taking a nap on the job? No, not all of them. He spied one standing in front of the cars, smoking a cigarette. He was so close that Clyde could smell the smoke, and he inhaled deeply, hoping for a little nicotine fix.

Should he chance a crossing here and risk being seen? Maybe he could slither across the road on his belly behind the cars. But that would be really chancy, and they might be out of their cars with their guns pointing at his head before he could spring up and escape.

The look-out yanked opened the car door of the first car and said, "Your turn. Wake up!"

The fellow in the car moaned and rolled out of the car, wiggling his neck around and yawning.

"What the...! You just started your watch! I didn't sleep a wink," he said.

"No, it's been two hours. You've been out like a light. We agreed on two hour watches. Nothing's goin' on out there. No sign of movement the whole time."

"Okay," the sleepy agent complied, and walked to the front of the barricade. The other agent climbed in the car and slammed the door.

Clyde didn't think it would be wise at all to scamper across the road. Maybe there was another way...maybe there was a culvert under the road to let the creek run into the river. He started looking along the road's embankment, trying to be quiet, but his feet slid down the embankment with every step. It was a quagmire of old garbage thrown out from passing cars, piles of leaves and rocks, and stumps from trees cut down by road crews along the side of the road.

Luckily, he saw a culvert pretty quickly. It was just big enough for him to squeeze into. He began crawling through on his belly. His arms and elbows were taking a beating on all the rocks that had washed into the culvert, but he was able to drag himself through it. He pulled himself out the other end, soaking wet and covered with slimy mud.

He found himself in a field of thick vegetation, long grass and shoulder-high bushes and trees, and pushed his way through them, headed downhill. The river must be close now, and he thought he heard rushing water.

He had been walking most of the day and he was tired again. He yawned, and rubbed his eyes. The night air was cool and felt good. He heard the noise of a motor, and looked up. In the distance, he saw something like headlights in the sky. A helicopter, he thought. Looking for him. He wondered if the other guys had gotten away. Except for Emmitt, of course. Emmitt was a goner. He shook his head back and forth. He knew where Emmitt was spending this day.

But HE was still free, still on the loose, and headed for the river. The helicopter circled away.

He made his way through the overgrown river bank and down to the water's edge. The water was high, and rushing dark and thick, chocolate milkshake-like, with barely a ripple. It had been a rainy spring,

Chapter 9: The Virgin Meets a Foe

and there was a lot of water coming through the watershed into the river. The highway passed very close to the river bank, so he had no choice but to attempt a crossing. He plunged right in, hands trailing in the waist-deep water, and hauled his body across the rushing river to the other bank.

He stumbled over someone lying in the grass there, moaning.

"What the heck…" Clyde sputtered, almost tripping on the body.

"I'm so tired. Don't think I can go on," whined the feller. It was Lester.

"Hey, Les! Where ya been?" asked Clyde, happy to see him.

"I dunno. All over them mountains, up and down, and every which way."

"But I thought you and the other guys were gonna steal a car," said Clyde.

"Changed my mind when I saw all the blockades and the FBI. Damn… You sure caused an uproar."

"What happened to the other guys?"

"They took off running next to the highway for the big city. I thought they were stupid, so I headed back into the woods." Lester sat up, rubbing his ankle. "What happened to Emmitt?"

"Couldn't keep up, got caught by the Hicks brothers."

"Crap," said Lester.

"Yep. Which way you headed?" asked Clyde.

"Gonna try downriver, keepin' low and quiet. I just can't handle them woods any more. I think I sprained my ankle."

"Well shit," said Clyde.

"Listen, no offense or nothin', but I don't want you goin' with me. If they catch us together, they'll give me twice as much time in the Hole," said Lester.

"Sure, I'll go upriver then," shrugged Clyde. He thought he would be able to hightail it over the old strip mines that he had heard were in that direction. There could be a distant town that might not be searching for him as vigilantly as the people in the area around the prison.

Lester stuck his hand up in the air, and Clyde gave him a hand up off the ground. Les said, "Good luck, Clyde," and started limping away downriver.

Clyde said, "See ya," and took off upriver, alone again.

Chapter 9: The Virgin Meets a Foe

The bulk of the river washing by on his left kept his attention so that he wasn't watching where he was going. He tripped over a rock, plucked himself back up, and tried to be more aware of his surroundings. Looking down, he saw what appeared to be a piece of coiled brown rope by his right foot.

He was startled by a loud chirring sound. He instantly realized that the rope was alive! It was a rattlesnake, and it was rattling at him!

The snake's broad head was upright, neck pulled back, ready to strike! Yelling, he jumped involuntarily backwards. The snake struck viciously at his leg, but its fangs slithered off his jeans to the side. He jumped backwards again, and the snake struck out once more, and this time practically threw its stout body at him. Somehow he was able to dance away from it.

He picked up a huge rock with both hands, and smashed it down on the snake's head. It was a lucky blow. The snake was stunned, and writhed and recoiled. He smashed the rock down again on its head, this time pinning the snake's head beneath the rock and grinding the rock on it with all his might. The rest of the snake danced and quivered in its death throes. Finally, all movement stopped. Clyde, however, continued shaking, breathing hard.

The snake was about 3 ½ feet long, a big one, he thought. It had dark brown bands on its broad back, and three inch long rattles of an intricate design. If only he had a knife, those rattles would be his. He had earned them by winning the battle with the snake, but he had to leave his trophy where it lay.

Reflexively, he pulled a piece of peppermint candy out of his pocket and slid it out of its cellophane wrapper to suck on while he calmed down. The wrapper drifted on the breeze into the weeds.

Chapter 10: The Veteran and His Dogs

Saturday evening and night

Night would be coming in a few hours. The rain earlier in the day had been a good thing for their man-hunt. Rain, sweet rain. Dog trackers like him loved the rain. The rain washed the forest clean of all its scents, and Clyde's recent trail was the only scent left to follow.

How he loved to run with his dogs! He was being pulled along over the hills as if his feet had wings. The key was to pay attention and stay focused on the dog and the terrain. He had developed this focus over the course of many daily training runs with the bloodhound pups. The one he had with him now was one of his newly trained hounds, and this was her first real man-hunt. The excitement was coursing through their veins!

Most people thought bloodhounds barked when they were after their quarry. But they didn't take the time to howl. They tracked the scent in the weeds, in the air, and on the ground. The scents of the men they were chasing became maddeningly imbedded in the folds of skin around their eyes and noses. They would chase those scents until they lost them, in a mad drunken spree across the hills, if he let go. But he would not let go. He was the alpha dog, and he had to keep control of the hunt with stern tugs and releases of the leash, with strong voice commands, and by observing the dog's reactions and making the final decisions as to navigation.

Sassy was an incredible, beautiful dog, although small for her breed. She was just 15 months old. Purebred and powerful, with a sleek reddish-brown coat. She was a ruby bloodhound, with coal black eyes sunk deep into pits and surrounded by blanket-like folds of heavy skin. She came from a long line of man-hunters, a noble breed, gentle, and loyal. People thought they were fearful animals and would tear into their prey, but they were extremely affectionate and loved people. The guards kept the dogs in a compound attached to the prison, and usually avoided taking them through the yard when the prisoners were out, so they rarely met. This helped them keep up the myth that the hounds would attack and eat anyone who escaped.

Guard Stockstill was being towed along by a larger male bloodhound, Elvis. They were right behind John and Sassy, due to Sassy's lesser weight and fleetness.

Before they got to the blockade on the highway, they ducked off road into the woods. They ran the dogs parallel to the highway until they reached where Clyde had descended down to the waterfalls. They found a white shirt button there, attached to a shred of blue prison shirt. The dogs moved in a quick, tight circle, and then suddenly pulled the men down the hill, tails flying high in the air like antennas.

Chapter 10: The Veteran and his Dogs

They ended up at a cliff next to a creek, and walked behind the dogs along the top. The dogs kept their noses to the ground, following the scent. Sassy led John to an overhang where it looked like Clyde had taken a nap. The dirt under the rock was messed up and moist. John rubbed some of the dirt between his fingers and smelled it. It had a distinct urine odor. Did Clyde pee in his sleep?

They climbed down a wash to the creek. The dogs nimbly scampered down the rocks while the men had to climb down with more caution. The dogs led them to the waterfalls, then they walked downstream some, and crossed the creek to an old roadbed. The dogs circled the area, doubled back on their trail, circled again. They were zig zagging abruptly, trying to spot the middle course of the trail, head and forequarters moving laterally side to side. John realized there was a pool of scent in the area, as if Clyde had been stumbling about in the fog. The dogs were definitely confused, but not giving up yet. At one point, they stopped at a patch of dirt, and began wagging their tails, and John knew Clyde had rested there.

Suddenly, Sassy was onto something. She was frantically pulling John now, and his feet were flying trying to keep up. He tripped once and tumbled, but then scrambled back up. He strived to keep his knees bent and his center of gravity low to avoid tripping again. His eyes searched the ground vigilantly for rocks and stumps in his way. Harry and Elvis fought to keep up.

Sassy stopped abruptly and stood in front of a patch of poison ivy. Her muscles were bulging under the skin of her shoulders and haunches, and she was straining to continue. Her tail was wagging quickly. She looked back at John, alerting him that she had found some kind of a clue.

"Sit," John commanded, and she obeyed, tongue hanging out and thick drool sliding down out of her mouth. "Down," he said when he reached her. She lay down, totally passive now, and awaited his next order. He bent over and rubbed Sassy's head, saying, "Good girl."

Harry and Elvis caught up and Elvis obeyed the same commands from Harry, lying down next to Sassy.

"What's up?" inquired Harry.

John just said, "Wait."

He used a stick to gingerly push aside the dark poison ivy leaves and found a pile of human excrement, still fresh, covered with a multitude of tiny blue butterflies.

John tried to wave them away, passing his foot over them, but they did not want to let go of their delectable food source, so he bent down and shook his hand vociferously over them. They fluttered up around his head, like little pieces of blue confetti.

"Spring Azures," said Harry, watching from behind him. "After the salt."

A local would never go into a patch of poison ivy to take a dump—that was just stupid. It had to be Clyde's. There were some torn off ivy leaves too, covered with shit and lying next to the pile. Clyde was going to be sorry tomorrow, when the itchy welts started up on his butt.

John was surprised that Clyde had taken the time to shit, but he guessed he just had to go. He wondered how long ago it had occurred. Reaching out one finger, he touched the pile delicately—it was cold. So it had been a little while since Clyde defecated. He wiped his finger repeatedly in some nearby wet grass, and then more fervently on his pants leg.

"Ick," said Harry, watching John and curling his upper lip.

John just rolled his eyes, saying, "Should have made you check it, asshole."

The dogs followed the scent back down to the creek bank where John allowed them to wade in a deep pool of water and cool off. They lapped at the water, and rested, tongues hanging out, but watching John for a signal to go.

The Virgin and The Veteran

John was hungry and thirsty. He pulled out some of his beef jerky from his backpack and amiably handed a piece to Harry. John chewed on his piece, letting the meaty juices build up in his mouth, then swallowing. Some of the juice slipped out the corner of his mouth and oozed down his long, silvery moustache. He didn't notice. Finally he took a good swallow of water from the metal canteen that was hooked on his belt.

"Up!" he finally said to Sassy and Elvis, and they jumped out of the creek, ready to go some more. He shook Sassy's leather harness, and said, "Find!" and away they went. Harry and Elvis followed.

They made their way around a bench and then over close to a power line cut, following the scent through the forest where Clyde had travelled. They reached the jeep road that eventually met with the highway at the gap, and ran across the road. They continued through the forest, next to the power-line cut until they reached the highway close to the river.

John was confident that he would have Clyde in his sights soon. The capture itself was usually anti-climatic. He loved the chase more than anything.

Chapter 11: The Virgin Runs

Saturday night and Sunday morning

"What was that?" said the startled FBI agent to himself at the highway blockade. He thought he heard someone yelling down by the river. The hair stood up on the back of his neck, and he felt excited. It was time to wake up Roger and get down there to see what was going on. He dropped his cigarette on the road and squashed it out with the toe of his black leather shoe.

"Hey, get out here. There's someone by the river. We need to go look," he said as he opened the car door and shook Roger by the shoulder.

Roger mumbled something about how working overtime sucked, and pulled his body out of the sedan, stood up, and plucked his gun out of its holster. "Shouldn't we notify headquarters?"

"Nah, take too long. Let's go, said Ben."

They beat their way through the underbrush down the hill and into the weeds. Roger had a flashlight, but Ben didn't.

"Where's your light?" muttered Roger.

"Forgot it," said Ben.

"Standard government issue. You're supposed to carry it at all times. Idiot," Roger spewed.

Roger shone their one light all about the riverbank, and still could see nothing. Ben, however, saw a dim shape running upriver on the other side.

"There he is!" he exclaimed loudly, pulling his gun from its holster.

This caused the fugitive to kick it into high gear, and the race was on.

Roger and Ben floundered through the rushing river, and were soon huffing and puffing as they endeavored to keep up with the shadowy shape sprinting along the trail at the water's edge.

They soon lost sight of the man and had to stop to rest. They both bent over, hands on knees, pitifully gasping for air.

"Where'd he go?" seethed Roger.

"I dunno. I don't see him any more," gasped the exasperated Ben.

Clyde had heard them yelling and carrying on behind him, and decided to give them a run for their money. It was a good flat trail by the river, worn and kept clear of underbrush, obviously used by local fishermen. He felt himself to be flying through the crisp night air, legs tucked under and pumping

Chapter 11: The Virgin Runs

up and down, the soles of his feet barely grazing the earth. He loved to run, always had. There had been very little chance to run due to the harsh terrain. Now for just a fleeting moment he could enjoy the freedom of really running. They would never catch him, he was so fast.

They were probably the FBI agents from the blockade at the road, and while they might not be very good trackers, they were probably good shots. His real adversary was bound to be one of the guards, probably the head dog tracker, Lieutenant Rankin. Everybody knew he was the best. He had rounded up every escaped con for the last twenty years, him and his dogs, and he had a glorified reputation among the prisoners. When they saw him, they called him, "Sir," a term they only used for a few people. Usually they called guards by their last name, like "Yeah, McPeters, what d'ya want?" They might get a swift kick, but they didn't care. But with John Rankin, they said, "Yes Sir, Lieutenant Rankin. Right away Sir." It wasn't that he did anything in particular to demand that respect from them on an everyday basis. But every prisoner dreamed of escape, and plotted and planned the day they would get out. And they knew that John was the one, the one they would have to deal with in the end. They respected that about him. It brought them out of their normal prisoner mentality. When they saw him, they stood up straighter, kept their eyes downcast, but paid more attention. If he came in the mess hall, they stopped their mind games with the guards, stopped throwing wads of white bread at each other, stopped annoyingly scraping their chairs. They got quiet and watched him furtively to see if he would notice them. If he looked their way, they ducked their heads. He was like a predatory bird spotting its prey.

Eventually Clyde no longer heard his pursuers behind him. He kept running anyway just for the fun of it. The trail soon gave away to a little drip of a thing, and began meandering through the bushes at the water's edge into several dead ends. He had passed the easy fishing spots and now was headed into the areas used by those wanting more of a challenge. The water was different here, with more rapids than before. The little trail came to another river crossing, and he had to cross back over to the other side, easily this time. The water was only up to his knees. The river upstream was narrowing, and he feared he might be entering a gorge where there was no trail.

Maybe the only way out was to try going up the wall of mountains to his left. He found a flat area where there were many concrete posts sticking up, and decided they were foundations of old buildings, possibly from the coal industry days.

He lucked upon a faint old trail going up the mountain. This would be his ticket out, he thought. It was time to attempt climbing the mountain again. He began ascending it, up into the cool night air.

Chapter 11: The Virgin Runs

There was a patch of pink flowers next to the trail, lit up by the full moon's light. He bent down to look at them, and was surprised when the flowers suddenly moved up towards his face. He jumped back, startled, and the flowers said, "Hey."

The flower patch slowly unfolded and stretched out some. It wasn't flowers at all, but a diminutive old woman getting up off her knees, turning around to face him. She held a short, pointed stick in one hand, and was wearing an old pink flowered housedress with big pockets and high-top tennis shoes. She looked up at him with sunken, faded eyes and said, "Smelled you comin'."

"Who the hell are you?" he stammered back.

She didn't answer, but instead said, "Are you gonna rape me?" She was leering at him with one tooth dangling in her open mouth.

"No, no, course not," he sputtered. She was looking at him fearlessly from a brown, weathered and wrinkled face. Her body was small and bird-like, with a hump growing on her back so that her head was pushed forward, with white hair puffed up on her head in disarray.

"What are you doing out here?" he said.

"Checkin' on the little men," she said. "Them Chinee folks love 'em. Helps 'em keep their women happy. This here's my 'sang patch. Grows all up the mountain, loves the shade from the big trees. I'm a hundert years old and I can't sleep worth a dang. So I come on out here to visit my 'sang.' They won't be ready to harvest 'til fall, but I like to check on 'em and all. Are you one of them 'scaped cons? I heered the whistle blowin' t'other night."

"Uh, yeah, I guess I am," he decided to be honest. She didn't look like she could hurt him. "You ain't gonna turn me in, are you, Granny?"

"Nah, not me. I wouldn't take away a wild thing's freedom," she said, looking him up and down. "But my son Walt, now, that's another story. 80 years old and still as spry as can be. Why, he works out with weights, ya know. He's jest down there a ways, tendin' to his still. He'd as soon shoot ya as turn you in."

"Moonshine?" Clyde's eyes got big, lusting after whiskey.

"Now don't ya go lookin' for more trouble. You need to git on outta here, boy," she said. "Here, I got somethin' for ya in my bag." She had a cloth sack around her neck, and she reached inside.

Clyde instinctively turned to run, half expecting her to pull out a gun. But she pulled out an old plastic bread bag, tied up on one end and looking lumpy from something inside of it.

Chapter 11: The Virgin Runs

"Here, you eat these, they'll do ya good," she said, proffering her bag to him with a gnarled hand.

The aroma released when the bag was torn open was heady. Something fried in cornmeal, he thought, mouth watering. He pulled out one piece, and it was crumbly in his hand. He popped it in his mouth, chewed, and swallowed. The middle of it was juicy and a little bit slimy, making his tongue feel scummy, but the outside was crisp and delicious with the fried cornmeal. He quickly ate the rest, at least fifteen of the yummy little balls.

"What is it?" he mumbled with his mouth full.

"Fried okra. Little pieces of heaven, dontcha think?" she said, beaming.

"Yeah, they're great. Got any more?" he said, swallowing the last bite.

"Nah, but you kin have this," she said, digging out some pitiful looking, wilted green leaves from her bag. "Have a good mouthful or two. And then rub some on your arms and legs. It'll change your scent some so them dogs'll git confused. You won't smell like piss no more."

He took a good bite of one of the limp leaves, and the garlicky taste exploded in his mouth. "What's this?" he asked, chewing and swallowing as fast as he could.

The Virgin and The Veteran

"Ramps. Ain't you never had none before?" She was incredulous. "Grows wild all along the river. Folks round here eat 'em raw, cook 'em in stews, eat 'em in salats, fry 'em up with cornmeal, eat 'em with bacon and aigs, can 'em for the winter..." She was going on and on, happily counting up the ways to consume her favorite food supply.

"I get it," he interrupted, realizing why she smelled like onions. She ate the stuff with every meal.

He rubbed some of the leaves along his arms and legs, pressing them hard against his skin and pants legs. Now he smelled like her. He dropped the rest of the leaves and told her, "Thanks, Granny."

"What's them rat bites on your arms, boy?" She reached out and grabbed his arm.

"Rat bites? Nah, I just got my body pierced by thorns, is all." He replied.

She squeezed his arm before she let go, and said, "You be careful up thar. Look out for them holes in the ground. Used to be coal mines up thar that was filled in, but they've kinda opened back up some places."

He told her he'd keep an eye out, and started up the trail beyond her, peering about expecting her son to be returning. She slowly got back down on her knees, back to her work, happily digging around in the garden of little men and humming to herself.

Chapter 11: The Virgin Runs

As he got higher on the mountain, what was left of the trail disappeared among the rocks. He didn't think he was on it any more. Some places were so steep that the mountainside seemed to be smack in front of his eyes, so that he had to haul himself up on all fours, hanging on to roots and trees. He was gasping for air, his chest heaving, his lungs burning, and he had to stop. He wrapped his body around the back of a tree in the fetal position so he wouldn't roll off the mountain, and lay there panting until he felt he could go on again. He continued in this manner for some time, crawling up, hanging on, curling around a tree to catch his breath, then continuing on again. At some point he realized he could stand up again, and not hold onto trees. The ground had leveled out some, and he looked around. He seemed to be on a small rise, surrounded by steeper terrain. Taking a good look at the ground, he saw a hole. There were small trees growing around it, rooting in the loose soil, tying up the dirt and compacting it. He held onto a tree and looked in. He wished he had a light. Must be one of those holes the old woman had warned him about. The dirt at his feet suddenly gave away, and he lost his footing, but he held tight to the tree and pulled himself back up.

"Damn," he muttered. "Kinda scary."

He thought he might throw off any dogs pursuing him by putting some scent into the hole, so he pulled the chicken bone packet out of his pants pocket and unwrapped it. He threw the bones in, and then he wiped the wrapping on the tree trunk before he threw it in too.

"There," he said. "That ought to keep them busy for a while."

He looked up at the continuing steepness of the mountain, and thought he would die before he ever got to the top. This place was his idea of trying to climb out of Hell. It was time to get off this damn mountain. Once again, he was foiled by the terrain, and decided to try and find an easier route. The only choice was to go back down the mountain.

He didn't want to go down the same way he had come up because he might meet his trackers or the son of the old woman, so he moved over to his left to a gully and started crashing down it, hanging onto trees to break his fall. It was a long steep drop back to the river, and he was getting beat up from hitting trees and rocks. He wished he had a parachute and could just let go of the earth and float gently down on the breeze. To Hell with these mountains!

Chapter 12: The Veteran Goes Alone

Saturday night

Sassy and Elvis were busily sniffing along the embankment below the highway, and were pulling the men to a culvert. Suddenly they were interrupted by two people coming up the highway towards them.

"Ho, whatcha doin' there, Sir!" John saw a man in a suit carrying a camera. His hat was pushed back on his forehead, and sweat was streaming down his brow. Long thick curly hair was tucked behind his ears. Behind him was a pretty young woman in a skirt and suit jacket, wobbling along in high heels. Beyond them was a blockade of black cars, with lights on and with men milling about in the road.

"Dang nab it," he thought. "Stupid reporters." They were messing up his search. He had to reel in his dog and make her sit at his feet. Harry also made Elvis sit.

"Wow, it's our lucky day! We were just about to give up and go find our motel for the night!" the man said happily, with a huge smile.

The woman walked right up to them. "Hi sweetie, oh, aren't you pretty!" She said in a high sing-song voice. She began to pet Sassy, and Sassy was loving

101

it, tail wagging furiously. Elvis got up and was pushing his head under the lady's hand, wanting his share of affection.

John let down his guard for just a moment, and softened. "She's the purtiest dog in the world," he said.

The man was asking questions left and right. "Are you looking for those escaped convicts? Are you following their trail? How long have you been out here? Can I take your picture for the paper?"

Before he knew it, the camera was flashing in his face, and the dang stupid reporter had taken pictures of him and his dog, and was asking him his name. Those photos would probably be all over the papers. He really didn't want that. He was just doing his job. Not only were the prison guards out here searching, but the FBI was out here too, and the helicopters circling overhead. And then there were these stupid reporters who thought they could do anything they wanted.

He reached out swiftly and ripped the guy's camera from his hands and whistled at his dog. She immediately came to attention and pushed past the woman and began running down the hill. He ran behind, legs pumping like shotguns, holding the purveyed camera in his free hand. Harry and Elvis also jumped into action, and tore after John and Sassy.

Chapter 12: The Veteran Goes Alone

"Wait! That's the Chronicle's property! Stop, thief!" cried out the reporter. The woman just screamed in horror and dropped her notepad as the dogs pushed past her.

He knew they would follow, so he yanked the film out of the camera and dropped it with the camera in the middle of the underbrush. Exposed to the elements, the film was useless now.

"Oh, boy, you're in a heap of trouble now," said Harry sarcastically, close on his heels.

"Shut up," snapped John.

The dogs stopped when they reached the river, and started snuffling in the underbrush, and circling around the area. They indicated that the river needed to be crossed, by the continual turn of their heads towards it. John and Harry urged them into the water, and they swam across it, towing the men behind them.

On the other bank, Elvis seemed to want to go one way, and Sassy another. It appeared that there were two trails diverging there. It was best to let the dogs do their work, and follow their noses. So John told Harry to go downriver with Elvis and see where that trail led. He followed Sassy upriver. They agreed that if one of their trails petered out or backtracked, they would join back up.

The Virgin and The Veteran

John and Sassy ran along upriver on the good fishing trail that he knew so well. The trail was normally full of scent from other people's passage, but the rain had washed most of it away, and Sassy was hot on just one scent—Clyde's. John figured Clyde had met up with another fugitive at the river and they had split up again. Clyde had naturally taken the most difficult route, just from being stupid and inexperienced. There was no easy exit from the mountains from the headwaters of the river. The river went through a narrow gorge and the relentlessly steep walls of the mountains collided with the water there. There were some old trails that led up, but it was insanely and inhumanly impossible for an inexperienced person to climb up those treacherous mountainsides.

John had climbed them many times, though, and knew every rock, every crag, every hole. He felt confident in his abilities, but still, it was night time, and it would be all too easy to make a fatal mistake.

Chapter 13: The Virgin Is Stuck

Sunday morning

The drop was so precipitous, he thought he was going to fall into the pit of Hell. He should have kept climbing up the mountain, as he had planned all along, instead of giving up again and going back down. Seems like he did everything half-assed, he thought.

Clyde was turned sidewise, jumping down the mountain, right leg first, then left, bracing on the left to keep from falling. Arms flailing, but trying to stay controlled. The drop soon became tumultuous, and he thought he would not be able to stop. He reached out to grab a tree, but his hands slid off the rough bark. It caused him to twist mid-air, and he fell on his side. But he didn't stop, he kept sliding down through the leaves. He desperately rolled onto his stomach and clawed the earth, hoping for something to grab to break his fall. He imagined the Bad Thing waiting for him at the bottom, mouth open, ready to devour him.

His hands hit a root and his fingers wrapped around quickly. He held on tight, but the root's fibers gave away from the earth, and ripped out with him hanging on. His hands slid off the end, and down he went again, but slower this time, so he was able to grab a large tree and hang on by wrapping his body around it, gasping for air.

The Virgin and The Veteran

What a stupid mistake! He should never have attempted going down this. It probably ended at a bluff over the river, and he could have died going over it.

His ribs hurt, and his stomach was burning from cuts. His shirt was all in tatters, as was his mind. He didn't know what to do, or where to go. Up or down, all directions were equally hard and equally distant. Hunger, fear, exhaustion, loneliness, all assailed him and made him cry out like a lost soul.

"Ayeeeeeeh!!!" he caterwauled. Let the man-hunters hear him and come and get him and take him back to the Hole in the prison. It was the safety of the Hole that he longed for now. Four walls, a concrete floor, a roof. No more walking lost in the mountains, no more falling, no more climbing, no more, no more, please, no more!

(Later he would remember this moment and weep at his stupidity...)

Wrapped around the tree, exhaustion overcame him, and he was almost lulled into napping. But there were bugs or something in his pants. His butt was itching so badly! He reached around to scratch inside his pants, and felt little bumps on his butt cheeks. Had that happened in the fall? Or earlier? What was it? Did he get bitten by some insect? He scratched until his fingers went numb and the bumps were oozing some kind of sappy liquid. He pulled his hand out and looked at it. Nope, it wasn't

Chapter 13: The Virgin is Stuck

blood. It looked clear like that liquid glue he used in grammar school. Then he realized what he had done. Poison ivy. He bet he had taken a dump in a patch of poison ivy.

Things could not get much worse. Stuck on Hell, and itching like Hell!

Chapter 14: The Veteran in the Hole

Sunday morning

John began the steep climb with intense trepidation. He had been up this mountain many times before, and it was always a difficult climb, no matter what kind of shape he was in. The mountain was mysterious and full of secrets, and even though he thought he knew it well, it always surprised him.

Today was no different.

He and Sassy followed the scent to the old coal mine halfway up. Its shaft had been filled in with dirt so that the bench was covered up and rounded out. But at the top of the filled in area, a hole had worked loose, due to rain and erosion. It had been open for a while, but it seemed bigger than the last time he had been this way.

Sassy went right up to the opening and sniffed the ground around the edges. She was particularly attracted to a tree above it, and snuffled around it joyfully. She looked up at John, finally, happily. It was her, "I've found it," look.

"What? Is he stuck in the hole?" John asked her.

She wagged her tail eagerly back and forth, like a lone windshield wiper in a storm.

Chapter 14: The Veteran in the Hole

John took four steps closer to the open mine shaft so he could peer inside, but instantly regretted it.

Down he slid into the abyss, as the side gave way. His legs gave out from under him and he slid on his butt, arms flying above his head. His hands flew open to break his fall and he reflexively let go of Sassy's leash. It was a drop of about fifteen feet to the floor of the dark pit. He landed in a huge pile of dead leaves, leftovers from last autumn that had fallen into the hole from the trees above it.

He was not hurt, except his pride.

He stood up and looked about, but couldn't see a thing. Looking up, he saw the small opening of light, and he could hear Sassy whining.

"Stay, Sassy! Stay!" he yelled.

He knew she would stay. She always obeyed.

He thought he should be able to climb back out, so he backed up a ways and started running. He hit the side of the shaft with both arms and legs flailing, climbing as hard and fast as he could. But the dirt beneath him gave way, and the rocks came loose and it was like a rockslide with him in the middle. He slid down on his hands and knees, back to the pile of leaves and dirt.

He tried again. And again. Then finally he lay in the leaves, weary from his futile exertions. What was he going to do?

He remembered the Vulture Tree that he had defiantly walked under. Maybe the old superstition held water after all. How did it go? "If you walk beneath a Vulture Tree, you will die a horrible death." Maybe his time had come.

The frustration of his situation overwhelmed him, and he got really upset with himself. Why couldn't he climb out? It didn't seem that difficult or that steep, but he just couldn't do it. He thought about the long hard winter he had been through, with the stress of going through his father's illness and death. He had put on a few pounds through that, and been unable to run the dogs as much as usual. And when he looked in the mirror, it seemed like his hair had gotten thinner. He was tired of dealing with it, so he shaved his head. Much easier to wash his scalp than the clumps of curly white hair that decorated his head. His long moustache had changed from blonde to white in a matter of months, too.

Maybe he was just getting too old for this job. He had never felt so exhausted before on a man-hunt, or so feeble, and now he had made a stupid mistake, totally unlike his usual self.

He guessed he was going to have to pay for it, because there were always consequences to stupidity. He didn't feel ready for whatever would come next. He sighed, thinking maybe Harry would find him. There was always that hope. Good old Harry.

Then he thought about Clyde still out there on the mountain nearby, lost, trying to climb it, exhausted. Maybe Sassy could get him to come back and help him. Unrealistic, but maybe it was worth a try.

"Sassy, I need help," he said, getting her attention. "FIND," he commanded. It was the one command Sassy lived for.

She wheeled around and was off after the scent again without any hesitation at all.

Chapter 15: The Virgin Takes Off

Sunday afternoon

There was a rumbling noise coming towards him from above. Clyde held tighter to the tree, and his heart almost stopped from fear. Was it some wild animal coming to eat him? He craned his neck upward from where he lay, and saw piles of leaves being pushed down towards him, with something big descending behind them. The animal was howling as it came.

It was falling too.

He saw in a flash that it was a dog, and it was going to come rushing by him. He would have one chance to grab it. He positioned himself tightly around the tree, holding on with one hand, and stuck the other hand out just in time. The dog came sliding by, and he grabbed its rear leg. The momentum almost yanked his arm off, but he held on for dear life. The dog was crying out in pain. He couldn't pull it up to him, though, and it was squirming and writhing in fear and the indignity of it all. He reached around with his other hand quickly, using his stomach muscles to hold onto the tree, and was able to catch the other rear leg and pull the dog back up to the safety of the tree, sitting up to hold onto it.

"Good dog, good dog," he tried to soothe it. "You about went over the cliff, didn't you? You'll be okay now, just sit still," he crooned.

Chapter 15: The Virgin Takes Off

The dog looked like one of the bloodhounds from the prison kennel. It was young, female, and scared. Clyde had always liked dogs, and held onto it with both arms around its middle. She licked his face eagerly, trembling.

He noticed she had a long leather leash attached to her collar and thought that it was a wonder it hadn't gotten tangled up going down through the trees and underbrush. Where was the person who was supposed to be holding onto the other end?

The dog would not calm down, no matter how much he tried to get it to settle down. It frantically licked his face and put its paws on his chest repeatedly, even though he kept removing them.

She writhed out of his grasp and started chugging up the steep mountain. He sat still, and she turned to bark at him, pawing the ground and shaking her head, as if she wanted him to follow. So he attempted to stand up, and started trying to follow her up the hill. It was so steep that he was on all fours, grasping every rock and root and tree to haul himself up.

The dog continued ahead, but periodically waited for long moments for him to catch up so she could herd him along. He grabbed her leather leash, and was going to let her do part of the work of pulling him up.

"Get along with you!" he yelled, trying to encourage her to pull him. She was like one of those Alaskan sled dogs, he thought. She would pull until her heart tore out of her chest. She was struggling with his weight, and slipping backwards. He didn't want to hurt her, so he let go of the leash, and managed the rest of the climb on his own.

They made it back to the hole in the ground. Thankfully, Clyde lay down beside it for a moment to rest. The dog, however, had other things in mind. She leaped on his chest, barking.

"Stop it!" Clyde exclaimed. Only thing to do was to tie her up to a tree, so he did. She wasn't happy with that, and pulled and tugged on the leash, even trying to chew it in half.

"Sassy?" Clyde heard a voice coming weakly out of the hole.

Sassy's ears perked up, and she gave out a loud yip.

Clyde rolled over and sat up, looking down into the opening. "Who's down there?" he said anxiously.

"It's me, Lieutenant Rankin. That you, Clyde?"

"Yeah. This your dog?"

"Sassy? Yes. Is she okay?"

"Sure, she's great. Wouldn't leave me alone. Herded me back up that damn mountain. I got her tied to this here tree. Whatcha doin' down in that hole?"

"I got too close, and the side caved in. I can't get back out."

Clyde's eyes bugged open at this. The big dog tracker was stuck in the hole! Amazing. How could someone with so much experience in the mountains have let that happen to himself? Ha! What a joke on him.

"Guess it's your turn to spend some time in the Hole, then," said Clyde slowly and vindictively.

"There's nobody else to help me. Can't you try to get me out?" pleaded John.

Clyde thought about this, with a smug look on his face. He thought he might have some bargaining power. "If I help you out, will you help me get out of these mountains?" he asked.

"No, Clyde, I can't do that." replied John from the shaft.

"Well, I've got to get going then. Somebody will probably come along eventually and help you get out," said Clyde, slowly. "Anyway, I can't think of how to get you out of there."

"Wait, Clyde. My dog. Could you unhook her from her leash? Give her a fighting chance."

"Okay." Clyde let Sassy loose, leaving the leash tied to the tree.

"Down, Sassy," commanded John.

Sassy lay down above the hole, head on her paws, and whined.

"Stay, Sassy." She quieted and settled down, ready to stay the duration.

"Go on, Clyde. Get out of here."

"Okay."

Clyde started walking away, and Sassy did not follow.

Chapter 16: The Veteran and the Rats

Sunday afternoon

After Clyde left, John settled back into the pile of leaves to try to rest up so he could attempt another run up the loose dirt and rock hill to get out of the hole. He thought he was healthy as a horse, and should be able to climb it. What was wrong with him that he couldn't do it? He felt depressed about it all and was mentally floundering in a dismal abyss of negativity.

He decided it was time to try to climb up one more time. He backed up as far as he could, and ran up to the wall, and started climbing up it using his hands as much as his feet. The dirt kept sliding out from under him, and he ended up on his knees again sliding backwards, but turned around so he was sliding on his butt this time. He was too heavy and he just couldn't get up enough momentum to get out.

He rested again with his back against the wall. Looking around, he couldn't see much due to the darkness that filled the void. The only light was coming from the opening up above. He could hear Sassy whimpering at the top, and was glad he wasn't completely alone.

"Sassy, STAY," he commanded.

The Virgin and The Veteran

He remembered his head lamp, and pulled it out of his pack. It was an odd contraption, attached to a leather harness he had fashioned into a sort of headband like the hippies of the 60's had worn ten years ago. He didn't like carrying a bulky helmet so he had made the headband. The light was hooked on it, with a wire that went to the battery pack on his belt. He put the headband around his head and tied it in the back, then clipped the battery pack to his belt and flipped the switch to turn on the light. A soft glow emanated out from his head. He swiveled his neck to the right to see a tunnel going off into the darkness. Something big scurried away down the tunnel when the light hit it, looking to be about the size of a possum.

He turned out his lamp to conserve the batteries. Nothing left to do but wait it out. Surely Harry or one of the other trackers would find him soon. He would just have to be patient. He was bored and hungry, and dug in his pack for his chocolate stash. Mmmm mmmm. Nothing like a candy bar chock full of peanuts and caramel chewiness to make you feel happy.

There was a noise to his right. He stopped chewing and held his breath. Was that a squeal? He dropped his half-eaten candy bar and turned on his headlamp again. There it was. Same big critter. Only this time it wasn't running away down the tunnel. It was just sitting there watching him. Big yellow-green evil devil eyes flickering in the glow of his light. Nose in the air, twitching as it sniffed his candy bar. Whiskers jiggling to each side of the nose. Big fat gray body, long tail. It was a rat, as long as his forearm, and as big around as a possum. It didn't seem bothered at all by the light shining on it. What would happen if he turned out the light? Would it come for his candy bar? Or worse yet, was it setting its sights on blood, his blood?

He quickly grabbed up his remaining candy bar and shoved it in his mouth, chewing rapidly. He might need the extra energy provided by those delicious calories, and he sure wasn't gonna share it with the rat.

He looked away for just a second to stuff the wrapper in his pack. When he looked back, it seemed like the rat had crept just a tiny bit closer. As soon as the light hit it, it stood there completely still except for the jiggling whiskers.

John heard a noise at the top of the hole and inadvertently looked away from the rat again and up. Sassy was scrabbling with her paws at the edge of the opening, whining. She must smell the rat.

"No, Sassy, stay!" he didn't want her coming into the shaft. How would he ever get her back out? "STAY!" he yelled.

Then he looked back at the place where he last saw the rat, but it wasn't there. He lowered his head so his light shone a path from where the rat had been to where he sat, and there the rat was about five feet from him now. It was a clever bastard. Its evil eyes glimmered at him.

"Coming to get me, are you? Well, I've got a surprise for you," he said, as he pulled his knife out of its scabbard. It was an eight inch long blade, sharpened to perfection, and had a handle decorated with pretty turquoise rocks. His father had given it to him, and he took good care of it. It came in handy when he was skinning out animals he had killed, and it would come in handy today for killing this stupid rat. He didn't want to risk a cave-in by shooting off his gun.

As he pulled the knife out, he looked down for a second, and then looked back up. The rat had moved closer still, and was now about three feet from him. There was a squealing noise from farther back in the tunnel. He threw his light back there quickly. There were three more rats in sight, and they were advancing. Oh boy, a war party.

These rats were fat, and enormous. What had they been eating? He guessed they must have a colony in the tunnels of the old coal mine. Maybe they ate whatever fell into the hole. He shivered a little then, just a tiny bit scared. They must be experienced killers, to be so fat.

He stood up, feet spread wide, arms to his sides, knife ready in his right hand, ready for battle.

Chapter 16: The Veteran and the Rats

The first rat was upon him then, leaping up at his belly. He whipped his knife inward and slashed it in half. It fell at his feet, in two pieces. No time to even squeal at him. Damn, he was good. This would be easy.

The squadron of three rats was on him next. Lunging and biting with open mouths. He could see nothing but teeth and whiskers. His knife stung them and cut them. They fell at his feet to join their dead friend.

Next a formation of five rats attacked him from behind. One of them succeeded in clinging to his back with its claws stuck into him. It was biting his neck. He threw his back against the wall and tried to knock it off, but it wouldn't let go. He reached around to the back of his neck and grabbed it by the back with his left hand, getting his hand bit in the process. He took his knife and eviscerated it, then slung it down the tunnel. There were two rats jumping up on his legs, eager for a feast. He cut their heads off and dropped them in the pile of bodies growing at his feet. Two more rats were leaping at his eyes while he was bent over cutting up the other rats. He kicked at them until he finished with the first two, then sliced off their heads as well.

The rats were coming out of the tunnel at him in droves now. This wasn't fun any more. He was beginning to feel like an old worn out warrior, and sweating profusely. He was killing rats left and right, as fast as they came at him. What would happen when his arm got too tired to swing the blade? Or were there simply going to be so many that they would swarm over him and hold him under while the mass of open mouths and pointy incisors chewed on him?

He realized that rats had but two functions in life. They lived to eat and they lived to reproduce. The male rats he was killing had massive dangling gonads. They must produce enormous numbers of babies, and they were all coming out of their nests to eat him. He was feeling so weary. How was he going to survive this massive onslaught?

Just then something came rushing and tumbling in a torrent of dirt and rocks down the slide into the hole, growling and barking fiercely. It was Sassy!

She was a whirlwind of anger. She leaped into the midst of the fray and whipped about in all directions lunging at the rats. She grabbed rats and slung them against the wall and broke their backs, and then she seized some more and broke their necks. She made the most horrible noises he had ever heard. She charged at groups of rats coming up the tunnel until they backed up, squealing and hissing, and then she pounced on them until they retreated down the tunnel.

Meanwhile, John continued valiantly holding his own against the other aggressors.

Chapter 16: The Veteran and the Rats

Finally Sassy succeeded in making all of the rats in her area run away. She whipped about and started attacking the rats that were still pouring out at John from the tunnel. Soon she had them backing up and turning tail. Still, even when not a rat could be seen, she continued growling and lunging after their shadows, like a crazed beast.

"It's okay, Sassy, they're gone. Good dog. You are such a good dog!" John tried to calm her down. She had protected her master, against his orders. She had never disobeyed him once since she had been trained as a pup. But he was so thankful now that she defied him this one time. She came to him and leaned her body against his leg, panting and drooling, eyes looking up at him adoringly. He bent down and wrapped his arms around her big head, fingers deeply embedded in the thick wrinkles of her neck, and hugged her.

"Thank you Sassy, thank you so much. You saved the day, girl. I don't know how much longer I could have held out. What a dog, what a dog," he crooned.

His hands felt sticky, and he pulled them away, realizing they were covered with blood. Whose blood? Sassy's neck and back were bleeding from bite wounds. He dimly remembered seeing her back covered with rats during the melee. His own neck and hand were throbbing. He reached around to touch the rat bite he had gotten on his neck, and it was bleeding too. He got out his red bandana and wet it down from his canteen and proceeded to swab off his neck and hand and Sassy's wounds. At least they would be somewhat cleaner.

He talked to Sassy while he cleaned her up. "You know they'll be back, Sassy. They'll all go back to their nests and get their cousins and aunts and uncles and brothers and sisters and grandparents."

Sassy licked his face. She was trembling a little.

"Here, let's rest a bit. Then I'll try to climb that danged wall again. We've got to get out of here," he said to Sassy.

Sassy shook her head rapidly and slung drool and blood all over John's face. He wiped it off with his already filthy bandana.

He wanted to sit down but the floor of the hole was littered with quivering, dying rat bodies. He kicked them into piles and sat with his back against the wall. The floor was covered with blood, but he didn't care any more. His hat had fallen off during the battle, and he picked it up. It too was covered with blood. He jammed it into the top of his pack. Sassy sat next to him, eyes attentive to any movement in the tunnel. John kept one hand on her neck, petting her, calming her. He was tired. He knew the rats would come back soon to make a meal of their dead comrades and him and Sassy if they couldn't manage to get out of the hole.

Chapter 16: The Veteran and the Rats

After a few minutes, he heard squealing coming from the tunnel again. Sassy growled and jumped up, the hair on her neck bristling.

John reluctantly got to his feet, saying to Sassy, "It's time. We've got to try to get out."

He put his pack on his back and got ready for his last attempt at climbing up the wall. Surely he would succeed this time. He had to.

Chapter 17: The Virgin Comes Back

Sunday evening

Clyde was thinking about the Hole in the prison. The first time they stuck him in the Hole was for not returning a prison library book on time. For that minor infraction, he got three days in the black pit. There was nothing in there but a hard cold stone floor, one thin blanket, and two buckets. One held drinking water, and one was the john. Once a day a plate of food was lowered down to him from the trapdoor, swinging crazily in a bucket, tied to a rope. He was starving every day, waiting for the food, and then when he got it, he didn't want it. It was a bowl of tasteless watery porridge, full of chewy lumps. He ate a few bites just to feel fuller, but about gagged on it. They didn't empty his waste bucket the whole time he was down there, and the stench and the accompanying flies were terrible.

He had spent many long days in the Hole during his years in the prison, usually for minor infractions of rules. Whenever they grabbed him and told him, "It's the Hole for you," he had to quickly get his head in order before they threw him down there. Time in the Hole was unlike regular time. He had to back off any agenda he may have had, and exist in a state of subdued isolation, as if he was alone in a spaceship in outer space. The inner workings of his brain always tried to make him give in to lunacy and do and say weird things while he was down there, but his will would hold him steady if he tried.

Chapter 17: The Virgin Comes Back

But it was never easy. Singing helped. He could never remember the words to songs he heard, so he made up his own words. The guards on duty made fun of his singing when they brought him his nasty dinner. That just made him sing the louder. They could take away everything but his singing, he reckoned.

No man should be kept in a dark Hole, he believed. There was no chance for reform there, no hope of escape, with nothing but the raw fear in your belly to keep you company. It could break a man down into a nub of a thing. The Hole was filled with needless suffering without a point.

If he left Lieutenant Rankin in that hole on the mountain, it would be payback for all the time Clyde had been forced to spend in the Hole inside the prison. But Lieutenant Rankin had never hurt him, or hurt anyone as far as he knew. He just trained the dogs and rounded up the escaped cons.

Clyde had to climb over a tall, downed evergreen tree. It had not been on the ground very long, because it still had green branches that bent when he tried to break them. He straddled it and looked at it thoughtfully for a long moment. It was about the right height and width, and it didn't look too heavy for him to drag.

Suddenly he made up his mind. It was a totally senseless decision, but it was clearly what he had to do. He grabbed the base of the tree under his arm and hauled it back up the hill to the opening in the ground. It was heavy, but manageable.

"Look out below! Stand back!" he shouted into the abyss, hoping Lieutenant Rankin would get out of the way.

Clyde waited a moment, then heaved the base of the tree into the hole. It hit the bottom with a thump. The tree trunk leaned against the edge of the shaft and led invitingly upward, with branches splayed out to each side. It was just tall enough to stick out the top of the hole about three feet.

"Can you climb up?" Clyde asked.

"Yes, I think so," he heard the Lieutenant say. "Come, Sassy," he heard next. Sassy was successful on her first try at scampering up the dirt next to the tree all the way to the top. Clyde shook his head in amazement. He wished he was light and quick like her. She greeted Clyde, then waited patiently for Lieutenant Rankin at the top.

Clyde thought he heard strange squealing noises coming from the bottom of the hole. He could see the top of the Lieutenant's shiny bald head and the thin beam of his headlamp as he pulled himself up through the branches. He would be at the top in no time.

Chapter 17: The Virgin Comes Back

Clyde abruptly turned and fled down the mountain, leaping over blowdowns like a deer being chased by a mountain lion.

Chapter 18: The Final Chase

Sunday evening

When Clyde yelled to stand back, John grabbed Sassy's collar and jumped backwards as far as he could, pulling her with him. The tree plunged into the hole right in front of them. It was like God had opened a doorway in Heaven, and sent down a stairway to him in the pit of Hell.

He climbed the stairway to Heaven by grabbing branches, setting his feet in the forks of the branches below, and pulling himself up through the fragrant greenery of the fir tree. Rats were beginning to mill about below him, squealing in a frenzy of joy as they plunged their incisors into their brethren, beginning an all-night feast. A few followed him up the tree, but he kicked them back down into the pit.

Sassy obeyed his order to come, and simply scampered to the top, no problem. John promised himself he would lose weight and get back in shape when he saw how easy the climb was for her.

Clyde had departed by the time John made it to the top. He threw himself over the edge, rolling a few feet to be safely away from the opening to the shaft. He stood up and untied Sassy's leash from the tree, reattached it to her harness, and they were back in business.

Chapter 18: The Final Chase

"Find," he said.

Away they went, chasing their quarry down the mountain. He followed the faint trail in the evening light, with Sassy easily leaping over trees that were blown down over the path, while he lumbered along behind. At the bottom, the river was darkly splashing along over submerged rounded rocks. He turned and ran upstream a short ways, until he found a good place to cross. He was ready to plunge into it and wade across, when he saw someone standing on the opposite bank. The sun had set except for a few fingers of light coming through the trees, shining down on a motionless human form. He told Sassy to sit, and she obeyed, wagging her tail through the dirt. He studied the form, trying to determine who it was and what was happening, and then he recognized Clyde.

He was taking a leak in the river. "Hey, Lieutenant!" he yelled, zipping his pants back up.

John pulled his gun out of its holster and cocked it, then aimed it. He should be able to bring Clyde down with one shot. He had him in his sights, and had his finger on the trigger.

Clyde must have seen that John was aiming at him, but he just stood there, waiting, as if challenging him to shoot.

John hesitated, breathing hard, feeling shaky. He couldn't pull the trigger for some strange reason.

Why had Clyde come back to rescue him? He didn't have to, and it probably ruined his chances of escaping. No con in his right mind would have done that. Every man for himself was the rule. Yet Clyde had changed the rules, and allowed John the chance to catch him fair and square. It didn't seem sporting to just haul off and shoot the guy. He wanted to catch him on even terms. The gun came down, was dechambered, and put back in his holster. He looked up and Clyde had disappeared.

"Come, Sassy," he said, and splashed through the black and green waters of the river, slipping and sliding on the algae-covered rocks. Sassy was strongly bounding across.

"John! Wait!" He heard Harry behind him on the riverbank. Harry and Elvis came breaking through the ripples right behind him.

When they were all safely on the other side, John said, "Where you been, Harry?"

"We caught Lester! Downriver at the old church. Mr. Big Mouth was worn out. Came along quietly enough."

"Did you take him back?"

"Nah, I passed him off to Wilson and Whitey, then me and Elvis came on up here looking for you. Elvis found your scent going up the mountain, but I

Chapter 18: The Final Chase

heard some yelling down here, so came to check it out, and here you are."

"Clyde's just ahead. But he's got nowhere to go."

Harry nodded. They both knew the only way out of the gorge was up a brutally steep and slippery passageway, which was an exhilarating slide coming back down.

The last rays of sunlight were caressing John's bald head. Harry noticed the omnipresent hat was missing, and said, "Where's your hat?"

"In my pack. Covered with blood."

"What the hell happened?"

So John sheepishly told him about falling in the hole, the rat attack, and Clyde helping him to get out.

"Clyde? He rescued *you*?" Harry was flabbergasted.

"Yep," admitted John.

"Reckon those rats are related to the ones that come up in the johns and scare the prisoners?"

"Probably. Makes the cons real nervous."

"Brown rats won't usually attack people, but you were in their home territory."

"You should have seen them. Those suckers were as fat as pregnant possums."

"Did you get any bites?" asked a concerned Harry.

"Yeah, a few. Sassy too."

"Uh oh..." Harry was looking really worried.

"What?!" demanded John.

"You got to be careful of <u>Streptobacillus</u> with rat bites if you don't clean them up proper. Nasty little bacteria that lives in their mouths, multiplies fast in a wound. You can get rat bite fever real quick— awful stuff with high temperatures, chills, headaches, throwing up, back pain that goes on for weeks," explained Harry.

John imagined tiny little creatures in his wounds growing and getting bigger and taking over his body.

All of a sudden he felt queasy and feverish, and said, "I feel sick." He stepped into the bushes by the river and had the dry heaves.

When he looked up, Harry's shoulders were shaking, and he was snickering.

"Did you just lie to me?" he accused Harry.

Chapter 18: The Final Chase

"Nah, but the hurling and fever don't hit for 72 hours after you're bit. Plenty of time to get you cleaned up after we catch Clyde."

"I should have know'd it. You asshole," John clenched his teeth together, inhaled, and then blew out a big mouthful of air, fluttering his lips in exasperation.

Harry was always taking advantage of John's hypochondriac nature, trying to make him think he was sick when he wasn't.

"Here, we can sterilize them right now," Harry said, pulling off his pack. "Here, I got some antiseptic in my pack."

"Harry, we got a fugitive to catch," said John, acting all huffy and business-like.

John and Sassy took off as fast as they could go uphill along an old railroad grade, and Harry had to race to keep up. The doctoring would have to wait.

Sassy and John ran to the bottom of an almost vertical slide that went up next to a wildly rushing side stream that joined with the river. Sassy hesitated, and looked back at John, questioning.

"We've got to go up that danged thing?" John asked in a tired voice.

"He can't be far," said Harry, catching up. "Come on." He leaped up the hill in front of John.

Every step up was torture. There was no path, just a muddy slide straight down through a hillside strewn with loose rocks. Sassy and Elvis were struggling to pull the two men up, from rock to rock. Elvis led the way, bounding as if in slow motion. They came to a level spot and were able to stand upright like real men for a minute. Then the perpetual uphill began again.

Just ahead, they saw their man, and the dogs erupted into feverish howling. Their tails were wagging so hard, they could have sliced cheese with them.

The men saw Clyde look back, see his pursuers 20 feet down the slide, look up to the impossible climb, and throw himself into a pile of dead leaves at the base of a huge rock.

In an instant, the dogs were upon him, their noses right in his face, big mouths drooling, tails pumping.

The chase was over at last.

Chapter 19: The Virgin is Tapped Out

Sunday evening

Clyde ran down the mountain as fast as he could go. No sign of the old granny woman this time. When he reached the river at the bottom, he turned and ran upstream for a short ways and crossed the river at a wide, shallow spot. He splashed into it and was soon slogging across the swirling waters in the late evening light. No sign of the Lieutenant coming after him, so he wondered if he had made it out of the hole okay. He stopped at the water's edge and looked back, but still no sign of him. He had to take a piss, so he did, right there in the water, standing on a flat rock, watching the arc of hot urine fall into the current.

At last he saw the Lieutenant on the other side, with his dog. Clyde quickly zipped up his pants, and yelled howdy at him.

The Lieutenant had seen him, too, and was pulling out his gun, and aiming it at him.

Could he shoot him from this far away? He thought so, but wasn't sure. But he bet that he wouldn't. Not after he had rescued him from the dark hole in the mountain.

Clyde stood there staring back at John, waiting, seeing if he would shoot. Didn't matter to him one way or the other. He just wanted to see if he would. Death was just another Hole, and he knew all about Holes.

The Lieutenant lowered his gun, and Clyde was exultant. Time to go, time to race to the moon. He would fly up the mountain and find his freedom after all.

He continued up along the faint trace of an old coal-mining rail bed cut into the river canyon. He soon came to a waterfall rushing down the rock face ahead and was forced to head up the impossibly steep hill trying to find a way out of the gorge. There was a madly rushing creek in his way, pouring forth gallons of water into the river. He couldn't cross it, so he turned and looked uphill. That was the only way out. He would keep going up. The hill was a muddy slide, and he had great difficulty standing, much less running up it. He made it partway up to a flat spot, then turned uphill again, back to the muddy slide, and heard voices coming after him.

There was no place to go. The uphill route was too difficult for man or beast, and his pursuers were right on his heels.

He had a vision of Jesus Christ giving up his life on the cross. He had seen this image a million times during his life, hung on walls, around people's necks, in churches, and pondered what it meant, and why a man would choose to give up and die like that. Maybe he had no other choice. Or maybe he knew something good was going to come from it, something worth dying for.

Clyde didn't think any good would come from his giving up, but he didn't think he had a choice any more. He had done everything he could, and now it was time to give up the freedom of the run. He threw himself under a pile of leaves and tried to cover himself up, attempting to hide for one last time. He knew the gig was up, though, and it was time to give up the race.

Cold dog noses were poking him in his cheeks, and slobber was dripping on his mouth. He heard the Lieutenant tell him to get up, and from some dark and distant place in his soul, he answered, "Yes Sir." He sat up, leaves sloughing off to his sides, and Sassy joyfully started licking his face. Clyde rubbed her ears and said, "Good dog."

It was over—the lost days and nights, the running and hiding, the inability to handle the terrain, the fear and exhaustion, the loneliness. And also, the joy of being free.

He petted Sassy and she continued to lick his hands and face, happy to see him. Elvis made his acquaintance, too.

Lieutenant Rankin handcuffed Clyde's hands in front of him, then thought better of it.

"We'll do this when we get to the bottom. You're not going anywhere, are you?"

"Nah, I'm done," said Clyde.

The two Lieutenants unhooked the dogs' leashes from their harnesses, took off the harnesses, and put everything into their packs, signaling to the dogs that their work was done.

"Let's go," said Lieutenant Rankin.

He started down the slippery slope, trying to hang onto trees and keep from bashing into the tumbles of rocks. Lieutenant Stockstill said, "Okay, your turn," to Clyde, so he began the slippery descent as well. He was rushing down the slope with Lieutenant Stockstill sliding right behind him. The dogs were freely dashing about, pouncing on them joyfully at every opportunity, trying to knock them down. Stockstill and Rankin were shoving them off, telling them to stop it.

Clyde was thinking that his days of freedom were done, so he sang his own version of Taps, mournfully. His voice echoed soulfully against the gorge's rock walls, and the dogs joined in, making a great din, their pack howling at the moon.

"The race is done,

Chapter 19: The Virgin is Tapped Out

Gone the sun,
From the river, from the hills, from the sky;
(hoooooooowwwwllllll!)
Night has come. Time to die."
(hooooowwwwwlllllll!)

At the bottom of the slide, they continued down the old mining railroad bed carved into the side of the gorge. When they reached the river, Lieutenant Rankin was once again about to handcuff Clyde's hands together in front of him, when Clyde said, "You know they're gonna throw me in the Hole as soon as I get back, and I'm awful hungry. You wouldn't have anything to eat in that pack, would you?"

Lieutenant Rankin's great bug-eyes bore holes into him. Clyde thought he was going to say shut up, and lock his hands in the manacles, but he didn't. The old Lieutenant sighed, pushed his gold-rimmed glasses back up on his nose, peeled his pack off his back and reached in, starting to pull something out. His enormous bald head shone like a dim headlamp in the last rays of evening sunlight.

Clyde's mouth began watering hopefully. All he could think about was chicken for some reason. Barbequed chicken, baked chicken, grilled chicken, chicken and dumplings, fried chicken, even bloody raw chicken. Please let it be chicken.

The Virgin and The Veteran

Lieutenant Stockstill suddenly put his hand on Rankin's shoulder, saying, "Wait a minute, I got something for him."

Stockstill took off his own pack, reached into a plastic bag inside of it and pulled out a long, scaly creature and threw it at Clyde.

Clyde jumped backwards and tripped on a rock, and the rattlesnake body landed on his chest. "AAAAAYYYEEEEEEE!" he yelled. Sassy rushed to him and grabbed the snake off his chest and slung it about, growling ferociously.

The rattle made a chilling revelry in the night. Lieutenant Stockstill got the dead snake back from Sassy's drooling mouth, and held it up to show it off.

"Crotalus horridus!," he declared. "Timber rattler. Tastes like chicken," he chuckled, and his bushy moustache twitched on his upper lip. "Found it down river from here, close to the bridge. Somebody must have had a battle with it 'cause the head was smashed up. I didn't have time to skin it yet."

"It's mine," spoke up Clyde, as he gathered himself back up from the riverbank. "I killed it."

"You did? Well, then, I guess this rightfully belongs to you." Lieutenant Stockstill laid the snake body across a rock and pulling his knife from its scabbard, sliced the rattles cleanly off the end of the snake and handed them to Clyde.

Clyde was ecstatic, holding them up to the fading light and turning them this way and that.

Stockstill started putting the snake back in his pack.

Rankin said, "That skin will make a nice hat band."

Stockstill said, "Yep."

Clyde saw John absently pick up a cellophane wrapper glittering on the ground and hand it to Harry to put back in his pack.

Chapter 20: Chicken is for Losers

Sunday evening

John watched as Harry played his joke with the snake on Clyde. Then he bent down to his own pack and pulled out a piece of beef jerky.

"Guess you were wanting chicken?" he said as he handed it to Clyde, half-smiling at him.

"Yeah," said Clyde, taking the beef jerky anyway.

"Chicken is for losers," said John, "You deserve better."

Harry agreed. "Chicken fat gets your gut all churned up and gives you the shits when you're running. Indigestion, heartburn, diarrhea." Harry was all about the details. His hat had fallen off somewhere, and Clyde could see the balding pattern where his remaining hair was receding from his egg-shaped head.

Clyde was chewing on his jerky, and mumbled, "I tried as hard as I could to escape."

Harry said, sarcastically, "Sometimes your very best just ain't good enough."

But John said, "Sometimes success just means getting your ass out alive. You did pretty good out there for a Virgin."

Chapter 20: Chicken is for Losers

Clyde was surprised, and said, "Thanks."

John offered Harry a cigarette then. Harry said, "What happened to your "Smell-Well's"? I didn't know you were smoking "Dromedaries" now."

"Upgraded for the chase," John said. "Here, take one."

"Nah, my wife made me quit," sighed Harry.

Clyde interrupted with his mouth full, saying, "That's sad."

"Here, smoke?" said John, offering the crumpled pack to Clyde.

"Sure," said Clyde, pulling out a smoke.

John lit up their cigarettes, and the two men stood by the river enjoying the ritual of smoking while watching the swirling water flowing freely downstream.

"Purty, ain't it?" asked John.

"Yeah," said Clyde.

Harry butt in, saying, "Oh, shit, give me one."

John proffered the pack to him, smiling. Harry lit up and inhaled a big draw, coughing immediately. "Out of practice," he said.

They enjoyed their smoke, then it was time to go. John cuffed Clyde's hands in front of his body, tying a dog leash to the cuffs. They put their packs on their backs, and told the dogs, "Come on." They started across the river, slipping and sliding over the slimy green rocks hidden beneath the surface.

Clyde had one last song in him, and sang it then, with great sorrow, his voice plaintive and blue. John knew he was contemplating the Hole and the dark times that were coming. But he also knew that with this man, there would always be another attempt at the run for freedom.

"My runnin' days are done,
So throw me in the Hole,
Throw me in the dark black Hole!
You can take my body, but not my spirit,
Down in that hell of a Hole."

EPILOGUE

Who is the hero in this story? Certainly not the escaped convict, Clyde. He had no plan, he got lost for three days, and he eventually gave up and was caught groveling in the dirt under a pile of leaves. (But in his defense, he did help John escape from the hole, he did survive, and he would try again.) The real heroes are the prison guards, John and Harry. They knew their way around in the mountains, had the confidence and competence to continue searching for three days, and succeeded in their mission. But the super-hero is Sassy, the courageous and loyal bloodhound.

Local prison guards teamed up with trained bloodhounds are truly an effective man-hunting machine. How could anyone expect to escape and get away from them?

Using bloodhounds to track escaped convicts takes many hours of training involving the dog and the trainer. I studied several books, as well as participating in a mock search and rescue. Sassy is based on a search and rescue dog I met and admired, a ruby red bloodhound with an incredible track record for finding her man.

The fugitive in my story, Clyde, follows part of the route for the Barkley Marathons, a 100 mile footrace held annually at Frozen Head State Park for over 20 years. He is captured in the beautiful but treacherous New River area where the race was originally routed.

The Virgin and The Veteran

Frozen Ed Furtaw's book, <u>Tales from Out There, The Barkley Marathons, The World's Toughest Trail Race</u>, was extremely inspiring and helpful in evoking the mood of the Barkley Marathons. A participant twice in the race myself, I understand its addiction. The first time I ran in the race, I failed to finish one loop in the time limit. I succeeded in completing one loop two years later, coming in ten minutes under the time limit. It was a high point in my life to have succeeded in this quest.

The Barkley Marathons has infected various members of my family as well. My husband, RawDog, has run in the Barkley, attended every Barkley, and built the fire and cooked chicken for hundreds of Barkley runners. Our oldest son, Danger, has run in multiple Barkleys. If you are a Virgin in the race, you would be wise to latch onto this Veteran and follow him Out There. He knows "every rock, every crag, every hole". He also has blown the bugle for many years to "Tap Out" runners who give up. Our youngest son, Kyle, has attended every Barkley since he was one year old, watching from his playpen. He has also tapped out runners with the bugle. Kyle created the incredible artwork for the cover of this book. A sister-in-law and her son, IV, have also completed a loop in the Barkley. I also must include lazarus, the creator of the race, as a family member, after over 30 years of friendship.

Epilogue

Some of the characters in my book may resemble Barkley personas. Other things have been included to mimic the Barkley, such as race t-shirt quotes, often told stories, the runners' fears, and my attempt to have the characters follow part of the Barkley route. The donated chicken for the pre-race meal has a special role in the book. The title itself comes from the racers' tradition of calling new runners "Virgins" and returning Barkley runners "Veterans".

I admire the tenacity and endurance of Barkley ultra-runners. They are like the adventure-seekers of old, who sought to create new boundaries to our world with their explorations into unknown territories. Barkley runners explore the mountains of East Tennessee as well as new territory within themselves.

Cathy Henn
January 1, 2011